The Puma

'It is not the tree that forsakes the flower.'—
ALEXANDRE DUMAS

Daniel Wiles

The Puma

Swift

SWIFT PRESS

First published in Great Britain by Swift Press 2026

1 3 5 7 9 8 6 4 2

Copyright © Daniel Wiles 2026

The right of Daniel Wiles to be identified as the Author
of this Work has been asserted by him in accordance with
the Copyright, Designs and Patents Act 1988

Typeset by Tetragon, London
Printed and bound in Great Britain by
CPI Group (UK) Ltd, Croydon, CR0 4YY

A CIP catalogue record for this book is available from the British Library

We make every effort to make sure our products are safe for the purpose
for which they are intended. Our authorised representative in the EU
for product safety is Easy Access System Europe, Mustamäe tee 50,
10621 Tallinn, Estonia gpsr.requests@easproject.com

ISBN: 9781800753686
eISBN: 9781800753693

CONTENTS

1. THE GOD OF THIS LIVING

9

2. THE PUMA

101

*Forsake me
Only me
Ruthlessly*

*Camouflaged
Under the rotting world
Judge me
Only me*

1

The God of This Living

I T was a good day when they arrived at the house. The man with the boy James upon his back as he had been for most of the trek through the Patagonian wilderness. He was a tall and gaunt man with long arms like those of a primate. His face was weathered more than his thirtytwo years would suggest. This was the culmination of weeks of travelling by land and sea. Home again. After all that time.

The man unhooked the cotton strap from his shoulder and swung the child around and set him down.

You can walk from here, the man said.

Where are we? Back in England?

No. I told you. Our new home.

It looked as though spring did not come at all in this place. The grass brown. The trees that edged the yard without leaves. The sky above grey and sunless.

But no Grandpa?

Just us two. I am sorry.

They went on towards the house. He had expected his father to appear. He knew it was impossible but still could not detach the place from the old man. He stood by the porch for a second and wondered whether to go now or sometime tomorrow. Could he sleep in this old house knowing what lay by the old apple tree?

The porch still held a bucket of dry firewood for the stove and the bench he used to swing on as a child. Nothing else. All that was needed. He watched James sit on the bench and push himself forward on its rusted chains.

Don't get too comfy, the man said. Need to unload the cart.

I'm hungry, James said.

Well. Let's sort the fire first.

When do the chickens come?

I told you. The man will bring them in three days.

James pointed to the old wooden shack that looked fit for storing tools and not much else. Is that their house, he asked.

Yes, the man said, turning. That's their house.

How many will come?

I don't know, he said, bending down to fetch two logs from the bucket.

He pushed open the door. The place was shrouded in half dark. The windows filmed with layers of green scum. He held the door wide open and let the light in and the place revealed itself. More so once he took the latch from the windows and threw them open. The man saw his childhood before him. The open kitchen and living room. The dining table with only two chairs. The small sofa by the door. The woodwormed beams overhead holding pots and pans on nails. The bathtub in the far corner. Nothing had changed. He went into the first bedroom. A single straw mattress in the corner. Cobwebs plagued every corner. He stepped back into the main room and to the stove and opened it and threw in the logs. He searched the drawer where the lighter fluid was always kept. Pulled it out. Still some left. He fetched the matches and looked down at the boy alongside him who stood watching and wondered what he was thinking.

After the stove was lit he went into the main bedroom, where another, larger straw mattress sat by a bedside table made of some dark wood and upon it old stacks of newspapers. He turned the one to read its date and it said *May 6, 1951*. Amongst the stacks were older ones still. 1947. 1944. 1940.

Who will sleep here? James said. He was stood in the doorway.

Neither of us. This was your grandpa's room.

They set up both beds in the other room and fetched their things. Food and cleaning supplies and new tools. Games for the boy. He could not find the football, though. The day was ending by the time they brought in the wool blankets. He had been cooking some pork chops upon the stove with butter and small potatoes that had begun to crisp. The cooking helped abate the odour of emptiness that had been lingering about the place.

Later that night they pulled the table near the stove and threw on some more logs and ate slow and talked about many things. The boy listened to his stories of the war and of this place when they were children and he watched with kind and bright eyes. This boy was the man's one and only success that remained in his life. He was speaking more and more with each day and asking more questions. And the man quizzed him in return.

So tell me what it's called when a player scores three goals.

Easy.

Well?

Hat trick.

Who is number nine?

The inside forward.

Sometimes he is ten too. That's your position isn't it.

The boy smiled. He was struggling with the chop. The man took it upon himself to cut the thing up thoroughly. After the boy put down his knife and carried on eating he said: Our forward is the best.

Who?

Dixon!

Just checking. You know I drank with Dixon before.

You were too scared to ask him for his name.

His autograph you mean.

The boy nodded. Placed another piece of pork in his mouth.

Father?

Yes?

Do you think I could be a good player like Dixon?

Why not? You just need to practise.

Do you think Dixon is better than Allen?

Of course.

He's better than them all, isn't he?

Robledo is a fine player.

Who's Robledo, the child asked. He spat out the strange word without the L and he wiped the spittle from his chin and the man corrected him and the boy said it again in the same way as before.

He plays for Newcastle. He is from this place.

I want to play for the best team.

I would be happy if you played for anyone.

But the boy would not play for any football team here, the man thought. His mind turned to what lay out there in the dark. The next day he would view it. He would introduce them.

He lay with closed eyes but awake for most of the night and behind them he saw the partially built house black like blotted ink against the golden twilight. The shadows of his family walking in and out of it to the temporary camp and his eyes were wide and hurt by the twilight and he was barefooted and emptyhearted. He felt the burning wood of the campfire and the wind that moved through the pines and the smell of sap from the chopped trunks and the burnt grass surrounded him.

He had decided to put off that same thing that kept him awake for most of the night. He instead took the boy fishing. The river moved calm and the air rushed into their faces and dried the water that splashed up from the bank and onto their jumpers. There was a bite to the air that fizzed the water as it broke about them. The man looked to the boy as he caught a fish larger than his own. A Reineta the size of a dinner plate. And how proud of him he was. He was ready to let him meet his grandpa.

They left the fish on the porch ready for grilling and went round the back of the house towards the small plot of land once filled with vegetables and herbs and small fruit trees. Now all that remained was the old apple tree amongst the dead beds. Behind the plot was a small wood and they entered it under the darkening day that grew darker under the cover of the trees and there was the grave of his father. He knew it to be so, for it was a simple cross of dead wood. No markings. About it rotten autumnal leaves from years past.

Here he is. Your grandson.

Hello, Grandpa.

A silence about the wood. He stared at the cross. Soon the boy became bored and began to walk around. The man still stared. Inside his head he spoke to the grave. Do you see him, the man said. Do you see?

ONE early summer's day they lay amongst the bones of a dead beech. Son upon father's back. The barrel of the rifle rested in a crook in the rotten wood. They both eyed its target. Son along shoulder and father along iron sights. Amongst the trees wandered a lone Huemul. It had been grazing for minutes. From here its massive ears and their recurrent flick were its only giveaway. It stepped closer.

Father, the boy whispered.

Be quiet please.

Are you going to get it?

It is too far.

The Huemul lifted its head. It stood in this way for what seemed like an age. The man's heart shook his entire body. A globe of sweat hung from the tip of his nose.

The Huemul stepped forwards and bent once more. The man fired. The crack of the rifle shook the forest. Birds burst out flapping. He let his head fall into his arm and let go of the rifle and pinched his eyes and then turned to James. He was taking the balled cotton from his ears. Close, the boy said.

The skies were white for weeks. He could not remember the last time it had rained. Could not be long now. Never was. This world has a way of letting you forget it is even there before tapping you on the shoulder, smiling. He made a promise to himself to remember it. Cherish the boy. Cherish this place.

They came to a clearing where the tracks disappeared and the land fell into an enormous valley carpeted by thick green forest. And on the other side the mountains rose. Sunbleached stone showed itself like bone through fur. This the farthest they had dared venture and it was by mistake. He did not wish to take James so far from home. He caught himself laughing. Far from their new home. Yet James had probably forgotten most things about England.

How he had already changed. The boy no longer the baby. His limbs had grown longer and his mousy hair was shoulderlength. His eyes dulled not blue but an ashen grey. The skull had begun to push outwards yet the remainder of the face sat still unshaped. His nose was unspoiled by this earliest of growth spurts. If he had any of his mother in him the man could not see it.

They moved with haste now. Father and son walking together as one creature through the forest's dying day. Pausing intermittently to scan the foliage ahead. The trees leant over them and birdsong smothered. They had gone too far. The knowing of it lingered in the back of his mind the whole time they had been following frightened tracks. And in his hubris he believed they could find it again even after the crack of the rifle.

Foolish.

Father?

Nothing, the man said, sniffing.

I'm hungry, James said.

I know. So am I.

He was becoming accustomed again to this home and its temperament. Its moods. But as spring grew to summer he did not find the same luck with fishing and hunting small game that he'd had when they first arrived. He had hoped this would be different. Next time it will be different, he thought. It had to be.

◆

Under the cratered pearl and amongst crying wind and wild grass the occasional calls of Culpeos cut. He eyed the grey land ahead. In between clutches of yet more dense forest, mountain peaks were surrounded by blackness. He judged his best guess of the way. He stopped and knelt in the grass as the wind pushed over them. He listened for the sound of that familiar water… Nothing.

They pressed on. Only mountains visible. And they still were but black stars' obstacles. He continued walking under a perpetual fear that the sound would never come. The two of them in this unending sea of grass and mountain.

But in an instant it was there: the rushing of the river. He followed it across the land while eyeing it. How beautiful it looked and how violent. The moon upon the water.

The night proved kind to them. He found and navigated the home trail, leaving the river behind. And in spots where under dense foliage the light failed him he used what had become muscle memory to walk the trail and his step, even though aching from the day, became more sprightly the closer he felt them gaining on the house. They came to a clearing and along a diverted dirt path through the small wood until they arrived at the small black building. Showers of stars burst behind. It sat there like some still wraith.

Footsteps on wooden floorboards. The boy stirred. The man opened the door.

Home, James said.

Yes.

I'm hungry.

It's bedtime.

He unhooked the cloth from each arm and the boy hung from his shoulders and he unlatched his arms and swung the boy around. Carried the boy through the dark into their bedroom and lay him down on the straw mattress.

I'm hungry.

Something little?

The man rose and said Too dark in here and stepped across the room with arms outstretched until he met the counter. He followed it with his hands and pulled out the drawer and rummaged about. His hands came up with the matches and he struck one. He lifted the match overhead and followed the beam past small things. Pots. Mugs. Dustfilmed frames without the photographs. He found the oil lamp and let the spent match fall and struck another and lit the lamp. The house awakened. Everything as they had left it. He fetched a biscuit from the bin aside the sink for James but when he went to the bedroom the boy was asleep. He sat down and set the lamp aside and slipped off his boots. He picked at the biscuit and watched the boy sleep. Lampflame shaken by the draught. The boy's infantile shadow quaked against the wall.

It was once his own: the same bed. The same age. He would lie with his eyes closed until his father went outside and then he would sneak out of bed and eye him through the window. His father sat on the porch alongside his mother, looking out on the yard. In that long ago it was still being cleared. Only half the size. His parents spoke in low mumbles. Occasionally raised their voices. A hissing sound. Then the voices would quieten again. He was always the only one looking. His siblings all slept soundly. Or pretended to.

They rose late. The boy always liked to sleep the entire morning away and it was not until the man began frying eggs that he was shaken from slumber. He sat up and went across the room to the table. The man eyed him over his shoulder. The boy gazed with hand under chin through the slatted window. The man wondered what he might have been looking at and what thoughts came with it. He followed the boy's gaze but saw only light.

You must have been tired, the man said.

No response. He flipped the eggs onto plates and went over to the table and set them down. Then he stooped and looked out of the window. At the yard's edge which formed the wood there was a fell tree.

Why didn't you tell me? he shouted.

He stood over the great reaching shards of the trunk. The rest of the tree lay across the edge of the yard and the chicken shed. He followed the branches and eyed where they had come to rest. The shed was tilted to the side with its roof broken in. He climbed over and ducked under the branches and attempted to open the door but it did not move. He placed his ear to the shed and heard nothing so he moved around the other side of the pens where the entire wall was crumbled. He whistled and shouted. Nothing. He turned to the wood and looked for any signs of the birds. Nothing. The yard had been cleared before his own birth for this reason. The trees fell every so often. He and his father were always cutting up fell trees from the surrounding woods. Or did they themselves fell the trees? He could not remember.

Inside the house he asked James, Did you hear it drop? In the night?

James looked up from his breakfast and shook his head.

He went to the drawer and fetched some keys and went outside again. At the rear of the house was the toolshed. He unlocked it with a large iron key and swung the door open. It did not need the lock for they had never in all these years had a thief, but he liked the peace of mind. He fetched two handsaws and returned to the house.

The eggs were in his mouth and a handsaw was in the boy's arms and they were back out again in the yard taking apart the fell tree. They went to work cutting apart the smaller limbs from the top and the more they removed the more visible the chicken shed became. The boy carried small bundles of branch up and away towards the house.

We will use it for the stove, James said.

Yes we will.

They worked through the morning and the early afternoon before resting upon the trunk. He had fetched some water from the well and they sat and drank and spoke about how long it takes trees to grow as tall as this one was before it died and the boy looked upon the man with wide curious eyes, those kind and beautiful eyes, and the man realised he did not have any photograph of the boy like the one he had of his wife he had kept in his pocket since they had left. Every now and then the boy pointed out some bird gliding above. The man looked up and squinted and hummed and sipped from his cup again.

By late afternoon there was but a trunk. The sun was high and sharp poking through blanketed cloud and the child was yawning.

Let's quit, the man said. Come.

They went into the chicken shed. Nothing there. He pushed open the door from the inside and it lit up the shed. Three dead birds. He lifted them by the feet and inspected them.

Where's the rest? James said.

Come on, he said, leading the boy out.

After plucking and preparing the birds he dropped one into a pot of boiling water over the stove and covered the other two and stored them in the underfloor pantry.

They went out into the wood and searched for the other chickens before darkness came again. They were not out for long. Found not even a sign. They were seven including the cockerel. All gone.

When he was the last of the children left at home he and his father would go to the lake downriver in a long, narrow boat. He watched the water push out from the sides of the boat in great folds. The steep grey bluffs. Raptors overhead in their floating like lazy planes. His father at the oars in his leather boots. Head down. Long black beard with stripes of white. The unpolished pipe lolling from the corner of his mouth. He lifted his head to consider where they were. Scanned about the water's surface. Then the bank. Then the surface again. Turned the oars in the water and let them drift to a stop. A clanging against the side of the boat. He knelt in the centre of the boat and reached down until his arm disappeared to the shoulder and then pulled. Up came the brown bob onto the boat and he pulled at the rope with both hands with a steady pace until the net showed itself. He inspected it for a moment. His shirt-sleeve black. A mumble. Then he loosed the net again. Shipped them with the oars to the lake's edge, where a collection of thin lenga beech lived.

Summer leaves. Full save one that reached with its spindled white limbs dead and dry. They checked the traps they had set a week prior. This the rare time they caught something. It was still alive. A large rodent. Who knew what kind. His father took the long thin knife from his belt and snuffed the life out of it. Scuffling amongst dead leaves. Then it was cooking over a fire. His father looked up at him as he turned the rodent on its spit.

You need not tell your mother, his father said. This is just for us. His father winked. He smiled.

Do you like living here?

Yes, Father.

You don't wish to go to the city? With your brother and sisters?

He said no. Or at least he thought he had. He admired his father then. Wanted to be like him. Wanted to live there his entire life. Why would he leave? He must have said no. At that time.

He went with James to the field. They harvested a few potatoes and carrots. He had expected more. There needed to be more. This field was supposed to be something he had greater control of. Out in the wild he relied on luck as much as skill. Now here he realised it was the same. Just because a piece of this land was carved out and farmed, that did not make it any less wild.

They stopped off at the apple tree that skirted the field and picked some early fruits. He let James eat the first. The boy's face tightened and squirmed. Better than nothing, he thought. He remembered the tree when it was shorter than the boy and when it first got its fruit. His father too had let him eat the first. He still remembered the taste. Sharp and bitter. He saw the taste in his own boy's face then. On their return to the house, he found himself blotting his eyes with his shirtsleeve.

That night they sat with stomachs growling as dinner cooked. The man rose and tended to the pot. Added the potato and carrot. Powdered mushroom and dried coriander went in next. He watched the boy messing with the catapult he had fashioned from a pair of abandoned gloves. It was falling apart and beginning to smell.

Eat well tonight, the man said.

James nodded.

Need the energy for tomorrow. We will go back out again. This time Father will get a deer.

The boy looked up frowning. How old is Mama?

What makes you ask about Mama?

James shrugged. You don't tell about her any more, he whispered. It was true. He had not mentioned her name for what seemed like ages. And all the boy knew was what he was told. Or could he remember what he was witness to as a baby? The man could not tell for he was too old to remember himself how powerful a memory is at age four.

It hasn't been so long. Don't you remember her?

The boy shook his head.

She will be twentysix this winter.

James dropped the catapult and placed his hands on the table and he looked strangely formal in his request. I want Mama, he said.

I told you before, it's impossible.

There is a horse field in Middle England where he and Olive lay together. How she looked afterwards. Reposed and serene. If she had had a shadow he could not see it move. The young sun showed itself over slate roofs and it was soft and warm. Before, they had been in a tavern populated with fat men and loud women. Smokefilled air. Clouds of grey stagnant and unmoving like low morning mist. The thick and choking stench of sweat, cigarettes and spilled lager. At first he did not see her. His hand simply touched hers upon the bar. A clash caused by a coaster grab. Her eyes were dark and black and her smile enveloping and he did not speak right away because he struggled to find the words. This meeting he remembered was made by something so insignificant that would in turn make a number of lives. Then on that horse field that could have been any in the country, he asked her:

What do you want to do?

She turned to him. Her face relaxed, a sleepy smile that barely lifted her cheeks. This is all I want to do, she said.

They gorged on heaps of food for the first time since arriving. Why not, he thought. The chickens were dead now. Wouldn't last long. The only thing he regretted was picking the potatoes. But they were already falling apart in the soup. He cut legs and wings from the bird before forking them out and ladling the veg and broth around the meat creating what looked to him a beautiful soup. He took a spoonful and blew upon it ten times and the boy mimicked him blow by blow. They did not speak much. The boy lifted his head from his bowl and grinned. He returned the smile. The man wondered how long they could last out here. How long it would be before the boy would want to leave as he had. Was this fairness? Was this kind? By and by these lands will consume you. Take your kin or let them go. Remember why you left and what you said to your own father: Who made you the god of this living?

Short nonsense dreams. Fanciful things. Her hair in dark spikes dripping seawater down the groove of her back. A hand upon his at the top of a hill. Things he had never experienced in reality. He knew not to pay them any mind. If he did then he would not be alive when he woke.

They attempted the hunt again. All day they tracked and waited. Hardly a word between them. He wondered if the Huemul had cleared out of these woods or were only another five minutes away, just waiting to be destroyed.

Learn from the past. You still have the chickens and their eggs.

But how long would they last? You could skin and dry and salt and smoke and store a Huemul. Make use of it for months.

Get fish instead, the boy asked.

You didn't like the fish before. And when we tried again it took too long. Remember? I think all the fish have swam away.

Where did they go?

I don't know.

The boy sighed and started making a clucking noise with his tongue.

We will catch a Huemul soon.

When?

Don't you trust me?

Yes, he said, yawning.

Yes what?

I trust you, Father.

Back home at the yard's opening he trained stares upon the stump of the fell tree where the trunk had snapped from it. Torn jagged like meat from the bone. He set James down and the boy sat on the trunk.

Will it grow back?

The man knelt at the stump and noticed knots of bloodred blisters and lesions spread about the tree where it had split. He ran his hand across it and felt it in between his fingers. Thick saplike stuff. I don't think so, he said.

The second chicken was eaten over the next few days. They ate it hot in broth, they roasted the legs over naked flame, they ate the white meat cold in the afternoon. These the days spent hacking away at the tree trunk into manageable logs. They rolled them up the yard and under the porch to save them from rain the man thought was sure to come any day, for he could smell it riding the wind.

It was not until they had cut and cleared the trunk that he noticed the others. He bent down and inspected each trunk in the surrounding trees. A handful of them wrapped in these same dark lesions like a wire around a bone.

James perched about fifteen feet up a tree. His left leg stretched and planted on a thick limb, his back against the trunk. He was armed with the catapult. His elbow cocked. The man eyed across to the other tree, where a squirrel scuttled in short bursts. Then it froze. The boy took his shot. A scratch amongst the wood. The squirrel jumped from tree to tree and fled.

Got one yet?

James turned to his father. Shook his head.

Come down. I have something for you.

The boy swung from limb to limb before dropping from the tree. He was so young still yet looked at home whenever arboreal. The man produced from behind his back a football. Dark leather casing. James's eyes lit up. You found it! he said.

Under the rubbish out the back. About time we had some good fortune. You can stay on the ground for a bit now.

The boy smiled. He dropped the ball and began dribbling it around the yard. The man joined him and they passed it to one another farther and farther apart with each kick. After a while the man set up a goal with two logs and they took turns as goalkeeper. The ball had deflated some but it did not matter and they played on until it got dark.

Dixon! the boy shouted, dribbling sloppily with the ball.

Shoot then if you're the best. I bet you can't score.

The boy shot. It trickled alongside the man and he fell over the top of it and let it go through the goal and he turned over and shrieked fake disappointment and the boy had already gone running off around the yard with his arms aloft. He watched the boy in this happiest of moods and imagined him in this way for all time.

They cooked the third and final chicken and the entire time the man did not see it as a gain. After this hen was in their stomachs there was no more to come after it. No new eggs. He felt their luck running out. Should they return to small prey? Try fish? He did not remember the last time it had been worth standing riverside for hours on end. The river did nothing for him but dredge memories.

He eyed James out in the yard. The boy was seeing how high he could kick the ball into the air. This would not last.

Under lamplight they sat with chicken soup. He

did not ask James any questions or test him on topics. There was nothing of animals on the continent, of the constellations and their names, of the captain of Aston Villa or what they had won. This night he could not think of anything but whether he would be able to kill a Huemul. Whether he was worthy.

After tea they played cards. Still their conversation did not move out of the words of the games they played. James yawned constantly.

Are you tired?

Sí, the boy said.

Sí?

James rubbed his eyes and hummed.

The father lifted the son and placed him in the bed. Aside him the lamp. He tucked James in under the blankets. His face half in dark, half in orange glow. The man parted the boy's hair from his face.

Where did you learn that word?

What word?

Sí.

I heard you say it.

When?

No response came. He could not tell whether the boy's eyes were open or closed. When had he spoken the word? Were there other words? The tongue of his childhood he had not spoken for years before coming back here.

He turned down the lamp and sat there waiting for the boy to fall asleep as he always did. Then after a moment a voice from the dark.

Father.

Yes?

What's your name?

You know my name.

Bernardo.

Yes. But in England they called me Bernie.

What does it mean?

I don't know.

Can I call you Bernardo?

You don't like Father any more?

I like Bernardo.

Go to sleep, the man said. Tomorrow we get a big deer.

He got into bed and slipped his boots off. Then the socks. He lay rubbing his feet. Where had the boy heard that word? Why was his name on the boy's mind? How much of what he thought he had shielded from the boy was the boy actually privy to? Outside the wind wailed with fury. It sounded to the man like someone was trying to get inside.

◆

The following morning he was woken by James vomiting in his bed. He held the boy by his shoulders and pressed a hand against his forehead. Slick with cold sweat. The skin cloudwhite.

Hey, he said. What is it? Come on.

He lifted the boy still retching and holding his stomach and crying. Took him outside onto the porch in his arms and set him down. James dropped to his knees and bent over and vomited again. Thick yellow plumes. The man squatted alongside. Rubbed the boy's back.

There, there. It will be all right. Get it up.

The boy retched again and again and he saw the squirming figure of fear and desperation not in the boy but in himself.

He fetched water and made James drink. Then he took him back inside and put the boy in his own bed. Pulled up the covers. He set down a small ceramic bowl. The boy still retched but everything was all sicked up. He sat on the bedside and ran his hand through James's thin mousy hair.

Rest today. Okay? You will be fine soon. Father will fetch you some medicine.

The boy's frightened eyes, desperate eyes. No, he said.

I won't be long. You stay here.

But—

You want to get better?

James nodded. The man pulled the covers to the boy's chin and tucked them in. I will stay until you feel sleepy, then by the time you wake up, I will be back. And with medicine. Okay? I will be back. I promise.

He went through the woods north of the cabin. The hand axe by his side. The tree he searched for was somewhere. He had seen it many times in that long ago.

He had walked these woods with his father. They followed trails created by the Mapuche folk. The sun was low and hot. The air thick and suffocating. He struggled to keep up with his father, who stepped with ease, cutting away any dregs of hanging branches or fastgrowing vines with a machete. They went down a reposed bank that led to a stream and they waded through it but he fell behind to lift some water to his face and drink. Then a crack around the side of his head. He slumped to the streambed and looked up. His father was leaning over him.

Your brother is sick.

He nodded. Sorry, he said.

This is not the time to worry about yourself. Always put family first.

Yes, Father, he said. Bernardo knew to always put family first. He was young but not an idiot.

They both went off farther down into the woods until they came to a small alcove of canelo trees. His godfather, Newen the Mapuche Indian, had showed them how to make extractions for tea. Bernardo always looked up to Newen, for he was like his own father but softer. He cared for and noticed all the little things: how a tree was thirsting, where to prune and in what way to gather without disturbing the natural order of things.

And even when he was a man with his own boy in this same place the canelo trees were still living. And more of them too. He took his axe and faced its blade towards the roots and struck downwards on it. Off broke narrow pieces of bark. They fell to the floor in strips. Then he reached up and grabbed a branch from the tree and pulled it downwards. He took his penknife and cut off a handful of its ovular leaves and watched them fall to the earth. From his pocket a cloth. He shook it out and laid it on the ground in a square and placed the leaves and the bark cuttings upon it and then folded it up at each corner to create a parcel. He rose again and stumbled against the tree. Too rushed. He let his blood settle and went to walk away but felt a hot surge in his stomach. Leant over and vomited.

On his return to the cabin he passed the stream. The foul taste of sick still lingered. He touched his knees and bent over retching once more. Looked down at the stream. Family first always. He walked through it and went on without stopping.

He boiled water over the stove and let the small parcel of canelo leaf and bark into the pot. He felt himself sweating at the forehead. Small tingling shivers along every limb of his body, coming in waves. He sniffed and stepped across the cabin and into his room. James was sleeping curled up clutching his belly. The man sat at the end of the bed and eyed the boy. This made him stir.

You came back.

Of course.

The boy held his head. I feel really bad.

The man reached out and placed a hand on the boy. I know, he said. It will be all right. I'm making medicine for the both of us.

Both of us?

I will have some too, so we will both be strong.

Are you poorly too, Father?

I'm fine. Don't worry. Go back to sleep.

Later that night he made the boy drink the last of the canelo tea and sat cradling him. James had sicked up the tea twice already. He hoped that this time it would be kept down.

Soon the boy was fast asleep. He touched his hand to the small forehead. Cold and dry. His own head was dry too but his stomach was in knots. He sat silently cursing himself for his own foolishness, for he assumed it was the final chicken that had gone bad. Foolish, foolish, foolish, he whispered to himself.

In the early dawn he shuffled from bed and walked out onto the porch and vomited. Hoped the boy was not woken by the harsh sound of it. He spat. Sat down on the porch in only his long johns. He looked out onto the yard reflecting the steely morning light. Another tree had fallen and the first few drops of rain had begun to fall.

Some days later they headed out holding dawn. James walked aside him. They went through the trees both fallen and standing. A woodpecker at work somewhere. He looked down at James as he sprung along the track as he always did when they headed out. Bernardo felt the excitement bursting from him with each step. The boy seemed much better now. The man had to make thanks to the land just as the Mapuche would wish.

They stepped out onto the riversplit plain that separated their stead from the wilder forests and mountains beyond. Blankets of mist rolling in the wind. The mountains rose from them like enormous stone arrowheads. To him these fixtures of the land were those that ruled it. They were the gods of this living and he had spoken to them and they to him and they had said Come and feed and live but it will not be easy nor should you expect it to be. You may die in this place and let that be under the mercy of the mountains and the forests and the lakes and the rivers and all that dwell between.

Where the river narrowed the figure of a Huemul stepped around the brush and drank from the water's edge. He knelt and pulled the rifle around and turned to the boy and pulled him down by the arm.

Will you get it, Bernardo?

He pushed forward on the bolt and chambered the round. It was far off. He was unsure. What was the animal doing out in the open? Until now he had only seen them in the forest. Here it was with head bent drinking from the water. A gift. He shouldered the rifle and eyed the sights. His finger met the trigger.

But he did not fire. The Huemul had bolted into the river and begun to thrash to the other side. Another form entered his sights in its place. Paused at the water's edge. A beige thing. Short and lean and striking. Its massive limbs extending into the water. A Puma. A thing he had only seen twice before, and only then when he was a boy. Other than that it was only stories. Told by his father and by the Mapuche. Fireside tales of monstrous creatures lurking out there in the dark, like spectres, looking for prey to sink their enormous swordlike teeth into. And only after the killing blow would the Puma make its presence known to its prey.

Bernardo guessed it was contemplating swimming after the Huemul, but the Huemul was already out of the water and with the wind. Impossible prey for either hunter. The man rested his cheek on the rifle again and trained the sights on the Puma. His finger curled around the cold iron trigger of the rifle. It would make almost as good meat for the two of them.

The shimmering coat in the sun. The tail aloft. Its massive paws resting upon the earth. Watching its and his prize escape. The Puma was missing a chunk of its left ear as if a half moon had been cut from it. What a magnificent thing. Even from this distance. It was some size yet not as large as he had remembered. And the Huemul was far too large for only one beast to feast on. Could it be hunting to feed its young? As he did himself?

Will you get it?

The boy's voice shook. The man turned and eyed him. Wide startled eyes. His mouth slightly open and his bottom lip wet like a beach stone.

He smiled at James and pulled his finger away from the trigger. No, he said.

He rose and lifted the boy and sat him on his back and headed off across the plains towards the forest. He already had the feeling any Huemul nearby would be even more difficult to hunt than usual. The presence of the Puma had made sure of that.

We will find it again, James said.

At first the man did not answer. What else could they do? Go back emptyhanded? Again? They needed something big from this world and they needed it soon. A victory. A lifeline. No. They could not go back. Not now they knew one was so close. When all seems lost, the man said, that is when you continue.

Afterwards he was quiet for a while. He realised what he had said sounded like something his father might have.

They trekked through the wet woods some half a mile away. The day was dark with cloud yet warm still. Soft smatterings of rain from the wide leaves above. On the forest floor the brush was dense and parted only by what looked like a large animal passing through. The man knelt aside a tree and amongst the roots found loose fibres of offwhite fur. Wet and dense but not with water. He lifted some of the fur between his thumb and forefinger and eyed it. Thin blood. Lifted it to his nose and sniffed before rising and wiping his hand on his trousers.

They followed the trail. Spoiled brush and leaves dead for years. More fur fibres. More blood. The duo quickened their pace.

They came to a dead tree fallen across the path. He grabbed James and placed him over the other side of its enormous trunk and then lifted himself up and straddled it and swung his leg over and dropped to the other side. He slipped on the soaking earth and went down a short decline before grabbing hold of another tree, this one adolescent. Behind him James stepped down with ease, laughing.

Funny, the man said. He got up again and reached for the rifle that had fallen against the roots of the forest floor. Amongst the roots was a huge deposit of Huemul fur. He looked back up the incline in the earth where he had slipped and saw scores of hoof tracks that had made the ground slick. He followed them with his eyes and met the adolescent tree. Imagined the Huemul striking it.

We're close, he said.

And they were. They came to a clearing in the woods where the Huemul sat on the earth, legs tucked underneath as though it was settling in for a long night's sleep. It looked unreal. Yet its stomach bulged and it breathed labouredly. It was less than fifty paces away and fled not. The man knelt. Aimed. Fired. The

Huemul jerked into the air. Its legs shot out from underneath it.

They approached the prey. It let out a breathy moan highpitched and fearful. The man unsheathed his knife and dropped alongside the Huemul and drove the blade into its side. The Huemul groaned. Its torso rapidly rose and fell. It did not die. Shit, the man said. He retracted the blade and stabbed the Huemul again. After a moment the head lolled to the side and its eyes closed.

He sat back and wiped the blade on his trouser leg and sheathed it again. Fetched the machete from his bag.

You got it! James said. Stepping around the animal and touching it.

I got it.

You killed it. It's warm. Why is it warm?

Its fur keeps it warm, the man said. He eyed the Huemul. Along its back leg and hind a great reaching gash splintered into two. He probed the wound and saw bone. His eyes widened. Thank you, he said.

Who, James asked.

The cat.

What about the cat?

It helped us. See? The man made a claw and drew it over the top of the Huemul's wound. Slowed it down, he said.

Should we share some?

With who?

The cat.

He touched the boy on the arm. There he stood. Blood of his blood. Warm. Kind. Even in the face of death.

Help me with this, the father said, bringing the machete down on the animal. We need to take it home.

AUTUMN brought a visitor. A man in a long poncho with high pointed hood. At either side of him two drenched goats. Their white coats offcoloured and splashed with mud. He hollered and took the boy and man from their fireside card game and out onto the porch.

Go inside, James.

The boy stood still. The man turned to him and repeated the words and only then did James go. When the visitor reached the centre of the yard he held both the goats with one hand and waved with the other. Bernardo tried to eye the man's face but could not see much of anything. The rain beat ceaselessly into the earth and bounced back out of black puddles. Bernardo turned back to the house and saw James peering out from the window.

When the visitor reached ten yards from the cabin he paused and pushed back his hood. A face Bernardo knew.

Jaime.

Hermanito, the visitor said.

They stood there for a while. Jaime soaked through. Bernardo watched him tie the goats to the decrepit hitching post. The rain stuck his thinning hair in spikes down his skull. It ran in rivulets down his face and into his squinting eyes. He looked not like Bernardo had remembered. Still, it had been so many years.

Quisiera salir de la lluvia, Jaime said.

Sí, sí, Bernardo said. He turned to open the door and the boy was stood on the porch again.

Do you know the man, Father?

He will come inside, son, see to the hot water.

Why does he bring goats?

Go on. And get him a towel.

The boy shot off. The man stepped up to the porch. Still Bernardo stood kneading the corner of his cardigan between thumb and forefinger.

Cuántos años, Jaime?

He was panting, wheezing. He was not an old man but must have been aged by something like work or war. Even in this dim light, he was shocked by the sight of his brother.

I don't know how long it's been. Twenty years?

Inglés? Por qué?

Why not? Spent more of my life in England than I have here.

No hablo, hermanito, no hablo.

El chico es inglés. We don't speak Spanish here any more.

Jaime let out a rasping laugh that caught into a cough. He bent over and spat into the rain.

I happy to see you, hermanito, Jaime said. He grabbed Bernardo by his shoulders as though he was but a child. Gran chico, he said, laughing.

Come on. Get in the dry.

They sat Jaime by the stove. Gave him a massive wool blanket to wrap around his shoulders. Towel about his head and neck. He hunched over clutching himself, sipping hot coffee from a tin cup. The boy had been knelt on the seat of his chair with elbows on the table and palms under his chin just watching Jaime with those eyes, those massive curious eyes. It was only some ten minutes later that Jaime returned the gaze.

Y cómo te llamas, chico?

He asks your name, Bernardo said. He leant against the countertop. Arms folded. Still confused. What had made Jaime come? And carrying those miserable creatures?

My name is James.

James?

The boy nodded.

Jaime sniffed. Raised his eyebrows and nodded. Pointed his coffee at the boy then back at himself. Tú y yo tenemos el mismo nombre.

He doesn't know what you're saying.

Jaime looked at the man and smirked. Tu chico es inglés.

Like I said.

He turned back to the boy and said, with great discomfort, You e me, same name.

James said nothing. Simply continued to stare at the man. The thrum of the rain on the roof. The steam rising from the kettle. All the while Bernardo stood thinking about how this man in his house had broken what otherworld he had created. It was the plain old earth again now, inhabited by all the rest of them. He gritted his teeth and felt a shooting pain in one of the molars and it was the one that always troubled him when he ate sweet things. Was this even his brother now, with all these years parting them? There is a stranger in the room. Watch how he moves. Scope his intentions.

Why did you come here?

Jaime lifted his head and eyed him blankly, like a dog uncertain of its instruction.

Por qué viniste aquí?

Hermanito. Escuché que habías regresado por un tiempo. Me preocupo por ti.

Don't worry about me. You weren't when you left all those years ago. Left me here. I didn't look for you when I came back. I didn't want to see you. Now you're here and I want to know why.

Why?

Why! Bernardo said. Por qué?

I say to you, Jaime struggled to say. Me preocupo por ti. Jaime's face straightened. He continued in a stern tone: Te traje cabras. Veinte años. Pensé que no volvería a verte.

Bernardo looked away. Tears stood in his eyes. I wished for that, he said. I wished I would not see you again. There's a reason I didn't come looking for you.

Qué estás diciendo, hermanito? Qué? No hablo. No hablo.

Bernardo repeated, this time in Spanish so his brother would understand.

The blanketed man sat back in his seat. Placed his coffee on the table. Bernardo, he said.

Bernardo! James said, mimicking Jaime's sounding of the word. Rolled R's. This was the first time the boy had heard it spoken in this way. Bernardo himself was reminded of the boy's presence and straightened his anger. He walked to the door and opened it. The rain's hiss was strong and serpentine. He worried for the goats. They were lying down now with their noses nuzzled and their vulnerable underbellies poking out. Ears flicking yet they would not hear if some predator came for them.

He turned back to the sound of movement. Jaime was dressing himself. Bernardo shut the door.

Stop. Stop. You can stay the night.

Jaime turned, half naked, and stared.

Again Bernardo spoke: Pasa la noche.

No me siento bienvenido.

You are welcome. You are.

Jaime was not welcome, but Bernardo could not set him back out there in that weather. Jaime did not even have any tent or canvas or tarp to shelter under while he slept and the man knew he would be the target of a huntress out on the plains with those roped meals alongside him.

Dijiste que deseabas que no hubiera venido, Jaime said.

Well, you're here now. I have seen you. That won't change if you stay. Sólo quédate ahora. Stay.

And he did. They spoke sparingly. Mostly it was Jaime speaking Spanish to the boy and the boy speaking English back. Bernardo sat in his thoughts. Blocked most of it out. When James was showing Jaime his catapult, the man tried not to think about the last time he had seen Jaime. Still he could not stop the memory forming and playing out and replaying itself again.

He was eleven. Raining for days. The roof had caved in under the swell. Water dripped into pots and pails splayed about the flooring. His parents rushed in and out. A team of horses stamped in the yard. Newen drove them. When visiting he usually spoke to Bernardo and brought him little carved figurines but on this day he sat hunched over in the rain like a depressed bird. Bernardo had no idea why he would not shelter under the porch. Furniture was being loaded onto the cart. His brother Jaime stood under a tarp smoking a cigar. Shoulders drawn up. He shouted to the men that helped load the cart. They threw on the last of the things and wrapped the tarp around them. The gathered water landed on Jaime and snuffed out the cigar's cherry. He threw it into the mud and shook the water from his widebrimmed hat and sheltered under the porch.

Then they were all on the porch. He, his parents, Jaime, and Lisa. They were talking and hugging. His mother crying. Then Jaime ran his hand through Bernardo's hair and looked down on him and said something like Hasta luego, hermanito. See you later, little brother. Or so he remembered. He could not tell whether he had made up what was said, but what he did know was that it was something simple, like something you would say to someone you are seeing that evening.

They watched the team take off down the yard and into the woods enveloped in rain and grey mist. His parents were already inside the house shouting at one another. He and Lisa stood on the porch. Dark skies for days. He collects them. Granitic and looming like endless mountain. And the woods beneath them. The world beyond unviewable, and his brother was gone.

The man rose early. A clear dawn. He gazed out at the woods or what was now left of them. He could see the lines of the mountains through them. Where the land dipped to eventually meet the river and he imagined this was all there ever was.

Jaime joined him. He was lighting up a cigar as he walked through the door. Good morning, the older brother said, shaking off the match.

I thought you didn't speak English.

Jaime blew smoke out into the wet morning air. Men in town. English men.

Do you remember when you left? I was standing here. See you later, you said. Then it was yesterday. And I feel like I don't know this man in my house.

My house. Casa? Tu casa?

He nodded.

No es tu casa.

Mother and Father are dead. Everyone else left.

Left?

Salido.

You leave, hermanito. I say to you, hasta luego. No see. Para ti, cruzaste el mundo. No hasta luego.

He did not respond. His brother was right. How could he complain? He had left for England without saying a thing. Not even hasta luego.

Te busqué por todas partes, Jaime continued. No le dijiste a nadie.

How did you know I'd returned?

Returned?

Regresó.

Sami. No sé por qué tú hablaste con Sami y no conmigo.

I talked to Sami because she told me about Mother, and Father, and Lisa. Ella me lo dijo por escrito.

Why returned, hermanito? Y con el chico?

Bernardo turned and looked at the house. He remembered how as children he and his siblings sat listening through the thin walls to their parents argue and swear. He remembered the draught. The feeling of the hard wooden floorboards. The cold at the tip of his nose. He turned back and spoke to Jaime only in Spanish and Jaime responded the same.

I came because I wanted to show Father.

Show him what? Your boy?

Show him that I could do it. That I made something for myself over there while he was stuck in this place.

He was never stuck here. This is what he wanted, little brother. He wanted the same for you too.

I remember a time when I did also.

Jaime cleared his throat and spat and rubbed it with the sole of his boot. So what happened? What happened between you two?

Things changed after Mother. He changed. Drank more and more. Turned vile. I was the only one doing anything around here. And only Sami and Lisa visited.

About that, little brother…

Forget it. You never got on with them. Why turn up to bury them? Check in every now and then?

I helped bury Father.

You did?

Jaime nodded. He took the cigar from his teeth and spat out some bits and replaced it again.

I would have come back, if I had known.

Sami didn't write to you?

I stopped opening her letters after a while. It got easier. Then when I came back, I visited.

She told you not to come here.

She did. I told her it was something I needed to do.

Even after you found out he wasn't here?

Who, Father?

Jaime nodded. He started to hold himself like he was freezing. Bernardo thought about offering him a jumper or a hot drink. Maybe they could talk inside. The boy would not know what was said after all. But Bernardo had been trying to remake that house, not have it be as it was. If it was full of Spanish again it would be the old house and all the pain would return.

Yes, Bernardo said. I wanted to show this place to the boy. Wanted to show him how we lived.

But it's not as you remembered, is it?

Bernardo sat on the old rocking bench and felt its slats snap beneath him. Looked down and picked at the paint that had once been white. Cracked and broken. Do you remember they used to sit out here and argue?

Jaime nodded. Mmm.

And you did nothing.

What would you have me do?

Bernardo turned and pointed to the far front window. I used to watch through there. And listen. I knew they hated each other.

Jaime turned. He held a resigned look in his face. You looked as your boy does now?

Bernardo rose and opened the door. James recoiled. He felt this place regressing. The boy listening to conversations he did not understand, as the man used to.

He stood again beside his brother, who showed concern upon his brow. He looked at Bernardo as if trying to talk him down from a ledge. This is no place for you two, he said.

We have been managing.

You look so skinny, little brother.

I'm fine. We're fine.

And you wanted to show your boy this place. How we lived?

The man nodded and said, You understand it fine.

He is dead now. You have been in this dying place too long. You can leave now.

Bernardo said nothing.

What are you running from, little brother?

You can have Father's room for one more night but I want you gone tomorrow. Rain or not.

Fine. Just promise me you will leave too.

Why?

Little brother, you know yourself this is no place for a boy. No place to grow up.

I know now how hard it was for Mother and Father to raise us here. How harsh this life can be. I'm sure James will learn it too.

I don't know what happened to you in England, but there's nothing for you here. Do right by the boy. You left here for a reason, we all did. Have you forgotten? Go back. England, or Aisén, Santiago. It doesn't matter. Just go and live in the normal world.

Normal world? What's normal about it?

Bernardo rubbed his palm against his cheek. He sniffed and dragged on his cigar one final time before throwing it out into the rain. He had made sense. And it was sense the man was not used to hearing, for he had not spoken to another adult soul for so many months. He knew this place was not forever for them. Just respite from everything else. Time to make sense of things, to decide where to move on to, but the void he had inside him from not being able to confront his father was still there. This place was still there.

Later that day they ate some empanadas Jaime had packed in tinfoil and spoke some more.

Did you go?

To France?

Bernardo nodded.

You fought for them, it is not even your country.

It was at the time.

Chile is your country.

Is it? Is this Chile?

They were wrong, Jaime said, taking a sip of the goat's milk.

About what?

The war. Everything. This place would have been better off with the Germans.

Didn't get rid of them soon enough.

Well. At least you came back. And healthy.

Bernardo touched his fingers to the back of his ear and felt along a ridge in his skull. Yes, he said. Yes.

It was the dead of night when he woke to a tapping on the porch. Not unlike the sound of his father's old walnut walking stick. He sat up straight. A cold spider of air scrambled down his back. He rose and felt his way through the blackness of the room. He opened the drawer and withdrew the matches and struck one. He fetched the lamp from its hook upon the beams and lit it. Held it towards the cold dark. He squinted. Made out the image of Jaime sleeping curled in his blanket. His body rose with the low snore he had been emitting since he had closed his eyes. He looked back to his own bed. The boy slept soundly. Outside a crying wind snuffed out Jaime's snores and clawed under the foot of the door and wormed through any available crevice in the walls. Through the window where it usually viewed as only dark there was a hazed steel glow. He made out the black spectres of trees towards the depths of the yard. He placed the lamp on the countertop and opened the lamp door and blew its light out. Again the tapping. Bernardo whirled around and eyed the window, whereby a swift blackness came shifting from left to right. He drew backwards and knocked the lamp over. Jaime snorted and shifted his sleeping position and began snoring once more. Bernardo felt his heart reaching from its cage. A thumping rabbit's leg.

After a minute he went to the door and opened it, slow at first. Its wood creaking at the frame. The cool air of the night creeping in and with it an almost silent murmur. Then he threw the door. Stepped out angrily. The dark yard was still. The wind ceased. He went around the corner of the porch. Nothing. He looked over the yard as he walked back around to the front door. As he went to step inside he heard a creaking. He turned back as the creak shifted to a snap, and then a flurry of breaks and scratches. A crack of indigo night sky pushed itself through a gap in the land freed by the falling of another tree.

They saw Jaime off early that morning under a low white sun. He waved as he went, goats in tow. Bernardo had refused them. Yet still Jaime's words stuck with him. The ones he spoke in the morning even more so:

Take the goats, please.

We don't need them. Got a Huemul not long ago.

Huemul? How many?

One.

Only one? How long ago?

We are drying most of the meat. Keeps well under the floor.

Little brother, if you won't take the goats then at least borrow them. They're good milkers. I'll come back next month for them.

We're good with water. The streams are good. The well too.

Mm. Go to the stream. Do not drink from the well. A shadow sits over this place. It feels not belonging to the real world. It waits to rot everything that sits within it. Remember what I said to you. Think of him.

Jaime nodded to the boy, then smiled, winked and clucked his tongue. Hasta luego, chico.

Bernardo thought of the dead trees cut open with disease. Of the failing crops. Of the chickens. Yet this was the reality of living from the land. Days without rain are long and many. It did not equal curses or shadows of the dead. He looked down at the boy.

Again they sought a Huemul. They strayed farther and farther from home the more they hunted the Huemul, which, by the final days of autumn, when the trees were but black dead fingers reaching in rigor mortis, was almost every other day. He found himself carrying the boy more and more. His tired bones did not allow so much trekking and climbing. Still they saw zero Huemul and very few signs of them having existed in the area at all.

THE first days of winter came earlier than usual. Steely suns low and cold. He stood upon hard earth. A bluff overlooking the river. The running was calm and constant.

Before, he had gone to the underfloor pantry. He had lifted the great hunks of meat from their aluminium container by their protruding bones and turned them over. Along each piece of meat he examined were scores of black abrasions and frothy grey blooms. The stench from the meat had shocked him. It unfurled in an instant, forcing him to pull his top over his nose. Still it penetrated. He had sat crosslegged watching the splayed spoiled meat spread about the floor for some ten minutes. His mind went in circles. He tried to remember the way he had been taught to dry, salt and smoke meat. He was certain he had done everything as correct as possible. He had sat there for a while. Quiet save the beating of his heart.

What is it, Bernardo? the boy said without lifting his head from the man's back. The boy mumbled as if the ceasing of their walk had woken him.

The truth was Bernardo had seen nothing. The river split the mountains and ran to the plains beyond. Weeks and weeks now and they had not found another Huemul. It was the same thing every other day. It was nothing, and this nothing made him turn back.

Why do we go home?

There are no Huemul here, or anywhere, Bernardo said. He spoke in a sorrowful voice as though he was confirming some elegiac conclusion on the world. And he was. Countless times now they came to nothing and this search for more large prey had only stopped them catching smaller ones. Rabbits, eels, Reineta, toads. They mourned the delight they had possessed with delicious Huemul meat. And on the trek back to the house all he could think of was what their winter would look like in this place.

On the walk home he bent over flipping stones in the stream looking for eels. Even these held themselves in secret. James hated them, this he knew, but the boy needed to eat. The mushrooms were dying. The berries few and far between. All crops spent.

He followed the stream for a mile and saw not a thing.

In the woods not far from the farm he checked the traps set about the shrubs and feet of trees. Each one as empty as the next, and with each discovery he felt his heart sink lower into his stomach.

On their way back to the farm he spotted a pair of squirrels scuttling across the branches, mating or fighting he did not know. He leant against a trunk. Levelled the rifle. Rested his cheek against the stock. They were fast. A fair distance. He chose one squirrel and followed it with the sights and fired.

Did you get it, Father?

No.

What will we eat?

We will find something, he said, not knowing whether it was true or not.

I am glad we couldn't find eels.

What?

I don't like eels.

Bernardo swung James from his sling and set him down in front. The man knelt before the boy and held him by the arms.

Do you like to go hungry? Do you like bellyaches?

The boy shook his head.

Then you will eat what I give you. What I can give you.

I don't like eels.

He shook the boy a little. I couldn't give a damn what you like, he said. I had no choice. Neither do you.

I want apples. And chicken. And eggs.

They're all gone. Now shut up.

Upon arrival back at the farm he noticed the trees. Almost every single one of them blotted black and bleeding some dark diseased sap. Some four of them were broken and fell. And beneath them through the woods and out onto the opening of the yard the ground was blackened and bruised.

Yet when they arrived at the house the trees were not on his mind, nor the failed crops, or the missing chickens, or the blackened grass, but sorrow for how he spoke to his child. He was sure things would become different with the killing of the Huemul in late summer, yet it was far more shortlived than he wished. It teased him. It gave him the taste of what their life could be, then vanished like wind on the river. Still he was shocked how quick he was to lose patience with the boy. It reminded him of those later times. The times when it was only the two of them.

The sun had not long set and not all the jobs were finished. They still had to bring in logs and finish clearing weeds that had grown over last harvest's plot. Bernardo was bent over hacking at weeds and wrapping the vines around his hand and yanking them from the soil. With the failing light each bit of weed became harder to spot. The sweat that blanketed the back of his shirt had turned cold. He rose and stretched. He heard his father's steps on the dirt. Slow treads like they matched the motion of the stars. He turned to face his father. The man with face of dark olive and hair of white. A face like weathered cowhide. He stared blankly at Bernardo.

What are you doing?

The weeds.

And the wood for the fence?

The berries?

Don't be smart.

What about you?

Me? his father asked, stepping forward. Bernardo could smell the whisky on his breath. Me?

Yes.

I do all the fucking work here, his father shouted.

So what am I doing?

You are taking the easy work. I created this place. Me.

You can have it.

The place fell quiet. It seemed the shouting had even shushed the roosting birds and the swaying of the trees. Bernardo attempted to walk by his father one moment, the next he was on the floor. Confused. His father stood over him. A great shooting pain in his temple.

A warm trickling down his cheek. He touched a finger to his ear. A ringing. Upon his finger the wet lacquer of blood. His father made off towards the house. As he walked he ordered Bernardo to do what he should have already been doing. Hauling the logs. The hard work. The real work. And he remembered those words many times over: I created this place. His father did create that world. And he was killing it as well. The god of this living gives life and takes it away.

He went out to the old apple tree. Black shrivelling about the branches. And beyond it in the dim spaces between the trees was the decayed body of his father in the earth with the worms below his simple cross. The trees around the plot stood like tombstones for the land. The pale grey etchings of mountains beyond like gates to a cemetery.

They slept hungry that night. He moved their bed aside the stove and added a heap of logs without bothering to count them. They would not need it tomorrow. James was soon asleep, but Bernardo hardly could close his eyes for longer than what felt like ten minutes. The low gurgling of the boy's empty belly disturbed him. The thoughts of his own childhood disturbed him. He too in those later days would go hungry often. These were the nights his father would beat him. Throw crops on a bonfire in a drunken rage. How could she die? he would shout. Over and over. Images of fire and fury. Sounds of pain raw and unmourned. Bernardo never could. His mind was only filled with thoughts of leaving. These days were the worse ones, the bitter ones. The better ones would always follow. When his father would be knocked out from the binge that came before. He could do a little fishing on the river. Gather some mushrooms. Wild plants and herbs. He remembered those days of calm water and birdsong. Still they were always filled with the fear of when his father would wake and do it all again. He could not let that become of his own son.

And when he did manage to fall into slumber he saw images of James upon a pyre of damp rotten wood. Unable to burn. And he would wake and clutch the child and wonder why there was some cold feeling. Some desire to have the boy ablaze in the first place.

It was already midmorning by the time they had finished packing their things. The man walked out onto the yard. A rucksack larger and heavier than the boy upon his back. He held the rifle slung over his shoulder and pulled behind him a slatted wooden sledge with the tarpaulin tent and bedding held inside. With the shorter days he could not say whether they would make it to the city without resting out on the plains. They had already set out too late. And with the nights growing colder and colder, he worried for the boy.

The boy lagged behind. He carried a small cloth bag tied with strings over each shoulder. It was not easy to make him do it.

You have to take some clothes, Bernardo had said.

I don't want to go.

We cannot stay.

Why?

This place is not good any more.

I like it.

You hate it.

James had sat down. Face in his lap.

Come on, the man had said, kneeling beside the boy. He had to make him rise.

You hate this place, remember? You hate eels. Remember, James? Those awful eels. No good. Let's go to the city and get apples, and chicken. Let's go, James.

And encouragement swiftly turned to anger.

Come on. Get up. Five seconds. Five, four, three, two, one. James. Get up.

He shook the boy.

Get up and pack your clothes. I won't do it. You make it difficult for me when we are here and difficult when I decide we leave.

And the boy had risen and begun stuffing the things laid out by his father into his small bag. They had been silent since. And in the silence Bernardo had not thought about their journey nor his hunger nor leaving his childhood home for a second time but only that the longer they stayed the more he saw his father in himself, everything good and everything bad.

Keep up, son, he said as they entered the dead wood that skirted the farm. It is a long way.

They walked on through the wood and heard the creaks of trunks threatening to collapse. No birdsong. No wind. No signs of life at all save these two defeated humans traipsing through the dead leaves and black grass like sick apes. The man was alone with his thoughts. Nothing to distract him. On regret and guilt. On failure and embarrassment. On sorrow for his father. How he had left him. How he never said goodbye. At least he still had the boy. It was the two of them against all else. Each of them the other's world.

By midday they were far out on the plains. They had been making good time. The boy had picked up a good pace, and Bernardo pushed him further. When he saw the boy sat down on a stone amongst the long grass he realised he had pushed on too hard. He untethered the sledge from his waist and dropped his bag from his shoulders and sat down next to James.

When do we get there? the boy said.

He blew a long breath through pursed lips. Scanned the land around. The highest peak that sat the other side of Aisén appeared large enough for him to make his estimation.

Not long now. About halfway there.

I'm tired.

I know.

Ahead, a treeline hugged the northern hills that rose from the plains. Dusted white. They were not even tall, he thought. And they usually did not show any snow or ice until weeks from now. The season had begun to show its promise and it was a promise of bitter cold fury. Of survival only for the determined few. The adapted few. It was a good time to make it to Aisén and beyond.

Come, let's keep going.

They had made it out of the long forest. It was only a handful of hours before nightfall. They stepped onto the edge of a bluff where stretches of flat rocky plain unfolded ahead. He turned eastward. This way, he said, but the boy was sat on the ground again. The life half drained from his body. Bernardo stepped to him and knelt.

Can you carry on? We are not far away.

The boy shook his head. Bernardo looked about the bluff. It was a good spot to rest, camp and move again with the morn. There was tree cover on one side, and the rise of the bluff on the other. But he feared the cold. How far would it fall in the night? He was sure they would last, but in what health? The boy's body was far too weak. They needed to get to the city before the end of day and he was sure they could do it. On the far side of this steppe there were the lakes, and the rise of mountains. And nestled in between was the city. Bernardo was furious at himself for creating the situation they found themselves in. How in his hubris he had thought they could live at the farm. The port called to him. It was his and their only salvation.

He strapped his backpack to the sledge and tied the boy's small bag too. Then he reattached the sledge to his waist, and lifted James in his sling onto his back and carried him and their things down the slope of the bluff.

As they came to the foot of the bluff there was a scratch amongst the wild grass. A smattering of adolescent elm trees quaked. It was no breeze. From the trees came circling a Puma.

Ears pinned back and mouth extended. Its eyes wild and ready to kill. It thrust forward like violent wind and

Bernardo startled and shuffled backwards desperately before falling over the sledge. He landed on his back, where the boy was still attached. He heard a slap against the rock. A blunt blow. The skull of the boy forcing itself into his back sent his chest rising. The man said nothing. No time to speak or even think. Get up, man. Get up. Bernardo scrambled back and rose to his feet as quickly as he could. The scratch of his boots on the stones. The Puma stepped closer. Swiped a paw. Its growl was magnificent. Its mouth held open looked like some organic trap with whetted yellow stakes. Bernardo threw his arms outwards and shouted Vamos, vamos! The Puma growled once more. Bernardo stepped closer, yelling. He shot a sideeye at the rifle lying atop the sledge. He bent to grab the rifle but the Puma's face relaxed. Almost as if it knew. Bernardo noticed the ear was half missing. An abhorrent creature. He paused for a moment. Remembered the Puma he almost shot weeks before. The Puma stepped back without taking eyes from the man. He grabbed the rifle. The Puma shot back into the trees and became but noise before rising up the far side of the bluff and into the distance. His eyes darted from the animal to the trees to the animal again. His breathing uncontrollable. His chest quaking. His ears felt stuffed with blood. He thought about going after it. About why it was here. Had it been following them? Had it had no idea they were there either? He stopped questioning when he realised James had not made a sound.

James?... James? he said. No answer. He snatched the boy from his back and turned him around. His head dropped.

He lay the boy down in the grass and shook him. James, he said. His voice shook. The back of his palm shook as he held it to the boy's mouth. Felt warm air. Bernardo exhaled. He snatched the canteen from the sledge and slapped water over the boy's face. Slowly James came to. He looked up at his father with those shy eyes. Bernardo, he said.

James. Thank God. Are you all right?

The boy nodded.

Are you sure? Nothing hurts?

My head hurts.

He lifted the boy up.

James stood up straight. Looked up towards where they had come from. Then he turned back to the man and said: Is this the city?

No, it's not. We are still some hours away. Come on. We must go faster.

But I feel sick, the boy replied. He could not meet his father's eyes.

Do you need to be sick?

James shook his head. Bernardo took his canteen and lifted it to the boy's lips. He recoiled.

You need to drink, Bernardo continued, pushing the water to his lips. The boy had a few sips.

Father.

Yes? What do you need?

My head hurts.

It will be all right. You had a shock. We will be at the city soon.

He threw the boy onto his back and secured the sledge and charged on. It was straight walking from here on until they reached the city. He prayed they would make it before nightfall. They had to. He tried to keep James talking, but the boy fell drowsier and drowsier the more they went on. He took to jumping and shouting the boy's name. Stay awake, he said. Stay awake.

By dusk they reached what he thought was the end of this stretch of land where the city would show itself nestled amongst mountain and river. He was wrong. There was but more hill and forest. He eyed the mountain he had thought signalled the city and realised it was not the mountain he had thought it was. Deep swells of anger filled him. He held his hands to his head. Gritted teeth. And all the while in his mind he could not keep from blaming himself. They should have rested atop the bluff. They had the position and the rifle to protect themselves. The Puma had taken him by surprise. That would not have happened if they had been camping. His greed had outweighed their safety. And they should not have even been there on this day. Should have left long ago. The boy's pain rested upon Bernardo's mistakes, pride, and now his shame.

The wind picked up and it had begun to rain. The boy stretched backwards and leant over the side of Bernardo's shoulder and vomited into the wind. He took the boy from his back and sat him down in the grass. He was cloudwhite all over and shivering.

The boy sat aside him as he set up the tent. The wind rocked them and sent the tarpaulin flying across the land. He went running after it. On his return he eyed the boy, who was lying down on the rainsoaked ground. He removed his coat and placed it over the boy while he finished making the tent.

That night he lay hugging the boy. James's shivers could not be swayed by the man's comfort. His head was swollen and red hot and his eyes almost vacant, drifting, pale as sunbleached bone. He softly shook the boy. Stay awake as long as you can please, James. Why don't we talk about Villa? Do you think Dixon would like it here? Dixon wouldn't sleep if his father asked him not to. You won't sleep will you, James?

He held the boy to his heart and prayed. Hail battered the sides of the tent. The wind raged. He wanted to scream. Instead, he ran his hand through James's hair and repeated himself for what seemed like hours, even though it was no use: the boy could not keep his eyes open, and his head only grew hotter and more swollen. He ran his hand behind the smooth of the skull and with it came a whine from the boy.

It hurts.

I know. I know. I'm sorry. Just try and keep speaking to me. What do you want to talk about? James?

But the boy moaned and let his arm fall. There was no keeping him awake. The man focused on his breathing. On matching it to the boy's. Slow and long breaths that eventually drowned out the hiss of the hail.

He knew the doctor in the city could help him. They just needed the night to come and go and they would make it before morning's end.

He wondered if it was still the same doctor. Or perhaps his son. In his memory he held a song of his sister.

His father drove a team of mules across the plains. He whistled the entire way. His mother was sick with worry. Still his father never faltered.

She will be all right. The doctor in the city is great.

You don't know that, his mother said.

I do. He has saved many people.

No. I mean you don't know she'll survive.

Above them the midsummer sun was blaring. Skydawdling scavengers hovered with anticipation. His father pushed the mules on. The girl lay in the back covered with a blanket. Her face was turning yellow. Her skull swollen. This failing face etched into his memory.

They made it to the edge of the city in what seemed to him like no time at all. And the doctor saved his sister.

With the first light of day pushing through the sides of the tent, Bernardo opened his eyes. He held a hand to the boy's head and felt coldness. His heart leapt. He sat up and turned the boy over. Said not a thing. He shook James by the torso. Softly at first, and then with more and more force. His hand that reached across the entirety of the boy's chest. Still he did not wake. James, he said, bending down and listening for his breath. Nothing. He rose again and shouted this time. Then once more. Tears fell from his cheeks. Quieter and softer again he called the boy by his name. But James did not respond.

He carried James in his arms along the riverbank. Left all else behind. The boy's head lolled over the edge of the man's elbow. His hair fell back, shifting in the wind. Bernardo could not bring himself to look down upon the boy. Through his periphery a smudge of bone white. The body in his arms cold and tightening by the minute. He kept his eyes ahead and walked.

He knew they should not have stayed as long as they had. His brother had given him his final warning. The place rotten from inside out. He had known of all the dangers sent forward by this world, this wilderness, yet in his arrogance he had believed he could be the one to change it, to make it his own. To become the true god of this living his father always fancied himself. He dwelled on this throughout the entire walk to the city. He thought everything through again and again. It was the only way his legs would carry on moving.

Rage took over him. He was furious at everything. His father, himself, the land, the Puma. If his father had not changed the way he had, Bernardo might have never left. If he had never left then the boy would not have been born. For all his faults his father could not be blamed for the death of the boy. Could he blame Olive? He knew she was laughing at him. He had thought the boy would be better for this life and away from her but that turned out false. Thought the move would be good for him and them both. It only moved them into more danger. Still, it was a sweeter thing having and knowing and losing James to have never seen him born. And if the land would have yielded to him and acted as it once had when he was a boy then perhaps they would still be there now. Thriving. And if the Puma had not run out on them they would be in the city now. The more he thought on it the angrier he became. It was he and the Puma. Both of them. He could not shake the fury. If only he could see the Puma now. He would tear its limbs apart. He could not see the purpose of it, this Puma's attack.

And he could not unsee it. The Puma with jaws dripping saliva and its demonic snarls and hisses. And the more he remembered and thought on why, the more he blamed the creature. This horrid creature that brought only suffering. And how once he owed thanks to this beast. And how he had spared it. Why didn't you kill it? Fool of a man.

By end of morning he was at the edge of the city, where the first few inhabitants lived on either side of the river. He set the boy down at his feet. Knelt down and laid his own jacket over the cold body. He could not bring himself to stand up. Not yet.

He looked out towards the houses about the river. Lines of traps floating across the surface of the water. On the banks wicker baskets and buckets. Out in front of the houses small plots of produce. Serenity lay down across the land. A place tamed by its people the right way. Back where he had come from, it was not his father who was the god of that living, or he, but the land. The land and all its children. The bluffs. The plains. The Puma.

H E took one final moment with the grave. Knelt in front of it with his hands clasped together as though he was pleading with it. Tiny spikes of green poked through the dirt. A weed or two around the crude tombstone. His brother had done a good job with it. Something he still had to thank him for. Although it had been weeks, to him it felt like yesterday he had arrived at this place and watched the boy lowered into the ground. And the hollowing feeling he had felt when it happened. It was his insides scooped out and dropped into a bucket. That night he slept aside the grave. Jaime, Sami, Lisa had left hours before. How the heavens raged with bright silent blisters. Furious at those below. He felt the chill of winter fold over him. If he had died lying in all that cold and all that dark, he would have accepted it. It would have been the least he deserved.

But he had not. Even though he had slept there for nights on end. And if not death then he knew there was nothing left for him in this place. His father was gone. His boy was gone. He did feel some pain in seeing and leaving his siblings once more, but it was incomparable to knowing he could not protect his boy. He knelt in the earth that bloomed new weeds.

Goodbye, James. I am sorry.

He rose and took one last look at the place his boy, a part of him, would reside. He was thankful it was not at the farm, with his father.

One late day in that long ago he was sat at a similar grave. The grave of his mother. He was a regular visitor. Always brought freshly picked flowering offshoots of trees or shrubs. He would lay them down aside the crude wooden cross without a name or year upon it. His father never saw the point. His godfather Newen had brought decorations: woollen adornments and a carved rehue to ward off spirits. But the old man accepted none of it. Don't worry, son, Newen said, I will find a place for the rehue. She will be safe.

On this day new buds upon the branches like tiny promises. Sprinklings of birdsong swooped about yet not a bird could be spotted. Only grey bulbs of cloud moved amongst the treetops that leant over him as if in an attempt to mock his sorrow. He took a short knife from his belt and unfolded it from its casing and set it down aside himself. He knelt over the cross and with both hands gripped tightly under the hilt of it he yanked it upwards. Soil sucked out and sprayed skyward. He placed the cross down softly and turned his head to the side to sneeze. When he turned back around his father was stood at the foot of the nearest tree. He looked apelike. His clenched fists fell almost to his knees.

What are you doing?

The boy knelt motionless. His muscles tightening. His heart beat like that of a frightened animal.

What are you doing?

Nothing.

I told you before.

Told me what?

His father stepped closer.

I don't want the name. No name.

Why? he said without looking up. He could feel his father's shadow aside him. Then the shadow upon him.

Enough.

He did as his father asked. Folded his blade and lifted the cross to return it to its hole, but as he did he felt the wind move over his ear. Then he was face down in the earth. What came next was unclear to him. A scuffle in the woods. A number of fists thrown. All he remembered was looking down upon his father's curled body.

His own breathing rapid. His father's slow. This was the last time he saw the man that gave him his own life.

He followed the stone path from the cemetery out onto the road. His two sisters waited there. The elder sister, Lisa, held a large military green rucksack. He approached them. The small one, Sami, held her hand to his arm. Quédate aquí, she said.

I can't stay. I will take a bus to the coast. And from there I will go to Liverpool.

Por qué no?

Every day I will be reminded of this.

Escucha, Lisa said to Sami. Él es inglés. She held up the rucksack to Bernardo. He took it and nodded.

Gracias, mis hermanas.

Escríbeme, Bernardo. Escríbeme.

He nodded.

He came to the edge of a small garden. Mountainous shrubs and flowers in a medley of colours. Down the short garden a wooden house painted daisy yellow. Jaime was up a ladder at work with hammer and nail at the roof above the porch. The valley returned echoed claps from the iron hitting the boards.

It's a Sunday, brother.

Jaime turned his head. He looked unhappy to see him. He turned back to the roof. Por fin te vas?

Yes. There is nothing else for me here.

Jaime stepped down from the ladder. Bernardo approached and held out a hand. His brother took a rag from his back pocket and lifted it to his forehead and rubbed it around the back of his neck.

I am surprise you return to me.

I wanted to do right and say goodbye this time.

I do not want.

I don't know when I'll be back. If ever.

Sé feliz, hermanito. Todo lo que quiero. Jaime smiled and shook Bernardo's hand.

I should have listened to you, he said.

No entiendo, hermanito.

Debería haberte escuchado. James todavía estaría vivo.

Jaime scowled. No seas estupido. Ven a tomar algo. He held out an arm to the door. Bernardo followed and went inside.

They sat at the kitchen table. Bernardo looked down. Jaime picked at something on the surface of the table and brushed it away with two sweeps of his palm. Crossed his arms and exhaled. He spoke without interruption and in clear and precise Spanish.

Sami and Lisa visited Father more often the more his health declined. Near the end they stayed in the house with him. Nursed him. He took us all there. Tried to make the best of it. For all the bad he did, he was a man of conviction. He took us and made that place some kind of living. For a while at least. I got word from the girls that he was ready to die, and so I went to see him. By the time I arrived he was already dead. But Sami and Lisa told me that Father could not speak sense. I assumed it was something he wanted to say to me, but no. He did not mention me. He did not mention Mother. Nor anyone else other than you. Of all of us you were the one who loved living in that place. Growing up there. It is a shame things ended the way they did. The girls told me he could not escape this feeling that he had let you down. And that feeling went with him—

Jaime ceased speaking when he looked up. Bernardo held a handkerchief scrunched to his face, his body lightly bouncing.

Outside they shared a handshake. Threatened a hug. It did not happen. Bernardo instead took a step back and sighed. Looked at Jaime for what he knew would be the final time. Then he and Jaime spoke on things he never would have expected.

Pumas malditos, he said. Fucking Pumas. I would love to kill them all. Vermin.

It is the wild, Bernardo said. Nothing you can do.

Nothing?

Like you said, there is only pain out there. There is nothing for me.

Way I see it, there is nothing for anyone anywhere but scars of what happened to them. And you cannot run away from yourself.

I do not run away.

We all try, little brother. Some go farther than others.

I don't know what else I can do.

When you returned with your boy in your arms, all you could speak on was the Puma. You wanted vengeance.

And you all talked sense into me. The stupidity of it.

You put our sisters' words into my mouth.

I need to forget it. Forget that thing.

Jaime held his hands up. Of course. Of course. I only want you to be at peace, little brother.

I am.

And if you are not, I hope you find it wherever you run to.

Goodbye, Jaime.

Jaime nodded sternly. Take care, he said. Spoke in such a way you might to a man you have only met a few times.

◆

The bus followed the new road towards Puerto Chacabuco. Waves of heat held upon the tarmac. A hot day made hotter by the broiling of the bus engine. It did not bother him, for he was swallowed by his thoughts. By his guilt and his failings. Now he was heading off somewhere else and he could not for the life of him understand why. It had become a reflex for him to recoil whenever some problem arose. Would he go back to England and be met by his failings there? To France and his pain thereupon where his blood lay buried underground? To some new place to infect others? This land had its fingers in him still. And those fingers were laced with guilt. He hated himself for staying as long as he had, and hated himself for leaving now.

The ship awaited him. Not many people around the dock. Trade goods were being loaded. He stared up at it from the docks and remembered leaving this place all those years ago.

A storm had ridden over the mountains and found itself atop the waves sending the boat lolling to and fro against its dock. There was no time to stand around and wait, so he ran onto the boat. Men threw things around and shouted. The deck rocked. There was a man leaning over port shouting at the loaders. Bernardo asked him if this was the boat bound for Valparaíso and the man turned and shouted at him, All hands. Put those boxes away, boy. Come on!

Am I in the right boat? he had said.

The man had furrowed his immense brow. The rain streamed down his face so much so his eyes could barely open. He grabbed the boy Bernardo and shoved him across the deck. Valparaíso, yes. Now come on. I'm already missing too many men because of this storm.

He had joined the small group of seamen helping load the boat. After they had finished loading, the storm began to let up. He went starboard side and looked out at the open sea. Empty but full of promise. It was to him what he could make of it.

When Bernardo as a man boarded this boat the day was much calmer. He would take the same journey he had all those years ago. From here to Valparaíso and from there to England.

There was hardly a soul aboard and everything was hot and sunsplashed. He walked across the deck and lifted his bag upon his shoulder. That same sea was blotted out with bright sunlight. Now he saw only nothing. A complete void without any promises. He turned around and walked back across the boat and viewed his homeland. The port. The small fishing village. The hills. Farther beyond was Aisén. His buried boy. Farther still were the mocking mountains. The ancestral world rotting and no undertaker to mind it. And somewhere out there was the Puma. And with it resided all of the man's guilt.

Two days later spring rains fell over the farm. They further rotted the fallen trees that infested the land around the yard. And the house itself had begun to sink in on itself. What a sad sight, Bernardo thought. Still, he did not view it for long before going inside and sheltering from the rain.

He found the bed as he had left it. Spared from the leaks. He dropped his backpack and checked the wood bin. There were but a few rotting logs remaining. Soft to the touch and slick with some strange mucus. He stuffed them in the stove and opened the drawer and fetched a little bottle of paraffin and squirted what was left on the wood followed by the bottle and then lit a cluster of matches and let them go into the stove. It hummed as it was engulfed. Instead of undressing to dry out, he put his backpack on once more and took another look around the house. He grabbed the mattress and brought it over in front of the stove. Then reached above to the wooden beam and shook it before sliding it forward, unlatching it from its support. He pulled downwards with force until it snapped away and made a hole in the roof. Pooled rainwater thrashed down into the centre of the house. He jammed the beam down the back of the stove and pushed it forward. The stove toppled over onto the mattress, sending its fire spilling out in a stream of flames. He went to the other side of the kitchen and opened the bottom drawer. From inside he heaved a small gas tank he kept for emergencies and threw it across the room. He did not stay to check his work. Instead he stood in the rain as the house burned. He waited for some moments before the gas tank blew and sent flames shooting from the windows. The roof caved in fully and every wall was carpeted with roaring fire too hot for the rain to extinguish. There he gave this world its funeral. Years overdue. He mourned it as he mourned his father. He hated himself for staying. Hated himself for leaving. Now he would do neither.

Under the cover of the southern forest, where the trees thanks to their distance from the farm held themselves in decent health, he unhooked his backpack. The clanging of the skillet and metal cup tied to the bottom of the pack. From inside he retrieved a cloth parcel of bundled metal. He put his backpack on again and untied the bundle and laid out the rifle in parts. Piece by piece he assembled the rifle and fitted it with an old telescopic sight he had traded for in the city. Then he rose and shouldered the weapon by its leather sling and took in a long breath before heading off into the wild.

2

The Puma

H E had been on his back watching the summer sun force its way through the cracks in the tarpaulin before it was snuffed out by the shadow of the Mapuche man. Bernardo sat up and held his palm to his brow. A dark shape still and quiet. He spoke to the man in Spanish, which he thought ironic for it was to both of them an unfavoured language.

You are the one I saw out on the plain, the Mapuche man said.

Yes.

What do you hunt?

Is this your land, Bernardo said, rising from his shelter and meeting face to face with the man. He was older. His hair greying in curls that sat on his shoulders. His skin like dried meat. His eyes big and black and close together and under them dark droops like used teabags. He wore an earthen poncho around a checked shirt and blue jeans.

No, the man said. I'm just passing through.

Bernardo turned and fetched the small pot he used to make coffee from the fire and set it down bubbling aside the logs. He looked up at the man and asked him if he would join him for a cup and the man nodded. They sat down together and made grunting noises until they were settled.

He lifted a steaming cup in salute to the old man and drank and then passed it across and watched him take it down. The Mapuche stretched his cheeks and sighed. Then he smiled as he handed it back. They did not speak much until the cup was almost finished.

Guanaco or Huemul?

Puma, Bernardo said.

The man lifted an eyebrow and took the cup from Bernardo and sipped.

You have been looking a long time?

Some weeks. I know it is around this area somewhere. I saw it twice before.

When I was younger we hunted Pumas. Me and my village. We were quite good. There are no Pumas here.

Bernardo finished the last of the coffee. He gathered a globe of saliva from his throat and spat it against the forest floor. Looked back at the man, who appeared proud of himself, like he had done Bernardo some kind of favour.

Don't know that, Bernardo said, stamping out the fire. He went over to his bag and started to pack his things. He always packed light for his daily sweeps. He aimed to walk some three hours away and back in different directions on the compass with each day.

I do, the man said, rising.

Bernardo grabbed the rifle that had been lying atop the bag and knocked a round into the chamber. What do you want, he said.

The man held up his hands in surrender. I don't want nothing. Nothing.

Be seeing you then.

It looked to Bernardo as if the man wanted to say something else a few times, for he sucked in air but nothing came of it. He knelt at his bag and fetched out the box of bullets and checked them as he always did. Counted twenty not including the two in the rifle. He had already spent too many. He regretted not buying more when he was in town. He placed the box back in the bag and tied it at the top and slung it over his shoulder.

Move, Bernardo said.

The Mapuche rose and walked on, his hands still out from his body.

Don't worry. I just want you where I can see you.

Bernardo watched him. Even though Bernardo knew he had no bag or weapon or anything. But what was he doing out there? Did he live nearby?

The Mapuche man did not turn around until they reached the edge of the tree line. Good luck with your hunt, he said.

All right then.

Most often he chose north, for that was always the area most populated with Guanaco, and this day was no different. The land widened to a great plain of long grass and giant prehistoric rock that looked left behind by giants. A deity's playground. A seemingly never ending valley stretched out in three directions, only dented by ancient river basins and pushed up by slopes themselves dwarfed by icecapped mountains in the far distance.

Along his walk he would stop intermittently to kneel and drink from his canteen. He would lie prone with the rifle and scope the land around for any sign of movement. On this day it took him until the sun was already on its descent to spot something. A lone Guanaco sentinel moving through the brush some two hundred metres away.

He followed it over a slope, where it had rejoined its herd. Some twenty of the beasts wandering and grazing. Still the sentinel pranced out from the herd to detect and warn. He squatted at a safe distance and fetched his lunch from the bag. A cold stew of rabbit and wild mushroom. The last of it. He sucked it from the mess tin and swallowed it without chewing.

He looked out on the Guanaco and wondered how much of the meat he could take from it back to his camp. Twennytwo bullets, he said aloud. Should really have bought more.

Nothing came worth shooting. He followed the herd in its slow movement eastwards until the light had begun to wane, and this he knew was his cue to return to camp and try again in the morning.

And it was during these return trips that the man's heart swelled in his chest and he remembered why he was out there in the first place. He watched the condors above blacked out like line drawings, not unlike those James had made from time to time. The mountains and the condors and the river. And in between them the black lines of he and the boy. Where is the house? he had said, to which the boy had not responded and only kept on drawing over the lines he had already made.

It was by moonlight he returned to camp and

found it inhabited by the Mapuche man. He had fixed a fire for himself and was grilling something over the top of it with a long iron rod. Bernardo gripped the rifle and quickened his pace until the cool metal of the rifle's barrel was pressed against the man's cheek. The Mapuche's hands lifted and they were orange in the fire's glow and the man shouted Don't shoot!

This place is mine.

I am just making you some supper. I am not here to steal this place. I promise.

Give me a good reason not to shoot.

You know me. You know me.

Who are you? Bernardo asked, noticing the panic in the man's voice. His hands began to shake. They were orange in the fire's glow. A cool wind blew over them and sent the fire laterally against the bracken.

It is me, Newen. It has been years, little one.

Bernardo lowered the rifle. The man looked at him through the sides of his eyes. His tongue ran across his dried lips and he went to speak but before he could Bernardo said, Newen. From Aisén?

Yes, it's me. Can I take my hands down now?

Bernardo let his bag drop to the floor, followed by his own backside. He pulled the rifle around his front.

Newen placed his hands on his knees and sighed. Imagine that, he said. Killed by my own godson.

What are you doing here?

I knew you would be back emptyhanded, so I prepared you something.

But why not say anything?

I thought you would remember me, but I suppose you were just a child when you left.

I remember you now. Of course I do. I just did not recognise you. You should have said sooner. I could have shot you.

I am becoming more dramatic in my old age. I have been likened to a boulder in the wind.

A boulder with a death wish.

Newen laughed. You have changed, little one. He reached out and grabbed Bernardo's shoulder. You are not so little any more.

You are not so young.

Here again his face held familiarity. Bernardo remembered the way his face creased when laughing. He remembered the sound of the laugh, too.

Your village? Bernardo asked. What of it?

The man waved a dismissive hand. Forget it, he said. I have not been part of that place for years.

But you were the Lonko.

And I got old.

That can't be the reason you left.

The man smiled and nodded slowly. It's that unbelievable, isn't it. Times are changing, little one. The wars saw to that.

Bernardo turned and placed the rifle down away from them. There was a silence. Newen turned the iron rod. It was two fish staked to it. Their skins crisping gold. When he let the rod rest again the wood spat and sent embers up into the night.

They ate with the call of the cicadas. Bernardo remarked on them being early and Newen said they were becoming more prepared these days. It's harder to live now, the aged man said. Everything is dying out.

Bernardo wondered whether this was the objective truth or just the worries of the man that spoke it projected onto those around him.

After they had finished eating they made sweet canelo tea from small parcels Newen had prepared. It reminded the man of the boy's sickness. Of him making a remedy. He struggled to see whether it was a small fatherly success or a failure for making the boy sick in the first place.

I should thank you, Bernardo said, sipping at the steaming cup.

No need. I always take some with me wherever I go.

No. I mean my boy got sick not long ago. I made him some of this tea and it helped him. I would not have known if not for you.

Newen's face brightened. You *do* remember me.

Of course.

I always loved you and your family. Your father was like a brother to me. He was sad when you left.

Bernardo cleared his throat. Avoided Newen's eyes. He felt a rage come over him. What are you doing here, he said.

Thought you could do with some company. What would you be doing right now if not eating the food and drinking the tea I made you?

Resting. Thinking.

Starving. A man cannot be with his thoughts like that. He needs company.

Who do you keep for company?

I have family that visit me. I live not far from here. I spoke to your brother, who told me what happened to you.

So that's why you are here. To check up on me.

He means well. You shouldn't be out here like this.

I will find it and kill it.

The Puma? You realise they sleep in the summer days? You won't find it until autumn or winter, and by then it will be long gone or dead itself. And then what was the point of your endeavour?

You know, Bernardo said, sitting up and straightening his back. I used to think you were wise. I thought my family respected you. Now I see they used you. Then and now.

Bernardo.

Thank you for the tea, he said, rising. He stormed over to the tarp shelter and lay down underneath it. He removed his jeans and rolled them up and used them for a pillow.

Bernardo.

You can stay here for the night, but don't let me see you by morning.

Will you listen for a minute?

A calm wind rushed through the camp. The spit of the fire. The call of the cicadas.

Go on then, Bernardo said. He was still lying with his back to the man like some petulant child.

I am only saying you are going about it wrong. I told you that you won't find the Puma this way. It doesn't mean you won't find it another.

He turned to face Newen.

You will have to leave much earlier, the old man continued. And learn different ways to track it. Allow me to show you.

Bernardo felt bad. Why help me? he asked.

It's the least I can do. You are my godson, after all.

I don't want to use you, Newen.

Nonsense. Now rest. We need to be up far earlier than you were today. I will wake you. Go.

Will you share the tent?

Newen shook his head and smiled. I prefer it here by the fire. Don't worry, son. Rest up. Tomorrow we hunt Puma.

The man bedded down for the night, and with a stomach full of tea and roast fish he soon found himself swept away into a deep slumber.

A mist clung to the hills that were white with snow and the sky like an enormous sheet of glacial ice and it snapped and cracked and through it fell the ruin of stars and he upon the hill and the boy upon the hill and he reached out but he could not grab the boy and aside the boy was the Puma and the Puma was the colour of the sun and he felt the snow melting on his skin and the Puma was sat upon the boy and the blood fell from its chin and the man reached out he reached out he reached out but he could not

When he woke the forest was still dark and it was not Newen shaking him from his dreams but the dreams themselves. His throat felt as if he had swallowed a spoon of soil. He rose and passed the fire that was now but embers, and Newen asleep aside it like a large dog. The man found a gap in the canopy above and viewed the inky starless sky. He exhaled and wiped his brow with his sleeve.

The late Liverpool sky had looked much the same. The sky that was when he had thrown himself from the Dutch merchant vessel *Bodegraven* on its final stop from Valparaíso in the April of 1937.

They worked loading boxes onto wooden pallets held unsteadily by ropes. Once they were attached to the cranes the cargo was lifted and swung from the ship down to the cobbled docks ready for transport. The swell pushed against the hull and sent salty spray over them. He looked over the edge of the boat. Dockers in their flat caps and suits thin as tea towels. The shouts of the men, the calls from the nightbirds. He took a few looks around before simply walking off with the passengers. Nobody called after him. How his heart leapt. Long gone were the green lands of home. He held nothing but the clothes on his back.

He stole along the docks amongst returning natives and ongoing aliens. The buildings lined the city like great brick mountains with yellowed windows. The chimneys sicked up white smoke against black sky. The smaller vessels chugged in the water alongside them as they stepped over the square cobbles and the cobbles were smooth and wet like cracked river ice.

They had started to funnel into a building he could not make out. And when he entered it he realised he had made a grave mistake.

It felt like he had closed his eyes for but a moment before Newen was waking him. He rubbed at his face and looked at this old man who knelt over him as a dark shape.

Do you breakfast, son?

What?

Before your hunt, do you breakfast?

I have nothing.

Good, Newen said, looking down at his wristwatch. The sun will rise in ninety minutes or so. We must leave now. Pack your shelter too. You cannot stay here any longer.

Why not?

Do you want to catch the Puma?

They left the woods in single file at a time when even the birds held their beaks. Newen ahead of Bernardo. The old man held in his belt a machete the size of his own arm and it lolled to the side as he walked.

Bernardo with rifle over his shoulder and bag upon his back. The two of them went on with an air of purpose. Bernardo did not know where they were heading or with what plan. He was sceptical of the old man. Show me what you know. Prove me wrong. Still he did not ask. The land threatened to light up with each step and he imagined what the Puma might be doing at that moment. Would it be on the hunt already? Or hidden away somewhere trapped in dreams, as he himself was not many minutes prior? Did it dream of killing James?

It will be on the hunt, Newen said, as if intercepting Bernardo's thoughts. The Puma love to hunt in these hours before the sun shows them in the brush.

Bernardo went on, saying nothing.

Within less than an hour they reached the edge of a bluff that sat on the lip of a massive valley Bernardo had not seen before. He had no clue as to how they had arrived there or how there was still land he did not know so close to where he was camped. Down in its basin the scant remains of a lake. It looked black in the dawn and almost swallowed by the land underneath it. Newen knelt and sniffed and pulled from his coat pocket a pair of binoculars and glassed the valley.

Guanaco over there, you see? Newen said, pointing with his free hand.

They were miniature dark shapes idling. What looked like hundreds of them.

Newen spat. The more Guanaco there are, the easier the kill. If there is a Puma in this valley, it will be somewhere over there.

The old man held the binoculars on different spots of land for some seconds before moving again. The thing about the Puma, he said, you won't often see them, but they will see you. They are perfectly adapted to this land, and we are not.

I don't care if it sees me, Bernardo said. I want it to see.

The old man rose with a groan and held Bernardo's arm for a moment and then went off down the valley. The evidence of a steel sun began to show itself behind the towering mountains that still in the middle of summer shouldered the last rags of snow.

They held up about a hundred metres from the herd and proned in the grass and the old man glassed the Guanaco and Bernardo looked around the steppe, its rises and mounds, its bracken plagued ditches.

So we are doing the same thing I have been doing for weeks, Bernardo said. Just in the morning.

If you want to know the movements of the Puma, you must know the Guanaco. How do they look to you?

Bernardo watched them. They were idle. Calm. They bent to graze and shook the morning cold from their coats.

At ease, yes?

Yes.

Newen handed him the binoculars. Over there, he said, pointing. Beyond that ridge. Can you see?

Bernardo considered it. Beige bracken lightening under the morning sun that crept across the steppe. There's nothing, he said.

Keep looking. Do not just follow and watch the herd. Think like the predator. Where would you hunt from?

As Bernardo was about to remove the binoculars a small head lifted from the brush. It peered towards the herd. He could hardly make out any notable features but knew straight away what it was. His arms tightened. His eyes widened. His heart picked up speed.

Do you see?

I see it.

They want the herd that is still. The large herd. Remember, the more Guanacos there are, the more chance they have of getting one.

Bernardo removed the binoculars and turned to Newen. It's too far, he said. Come on.

Wait, the old man said, tapping Bernardo's arm with the back of his hand. Pass me those. Train your rifle on it.

We need to catch up with it. What if it runs?

As long as this herd is still, we wait.

The sun had almost reached them and the herd remained still. They had kept their sights on the Puma as it shifted into view and away again amongst the slight rises and dips of the steppe. He pushed on the bolt and chambered a round. No clear shot.

Where is the sentinel? Bernardo said.

To the east. He has brought them to the wrong spot, that's for certain. He has no idea what's coming.

The Puma pushed closer. It seemed to glide amongst the brush. Only its head rising every now and then. Its ears flickering. Were they the same scarred ones? Bernardo kept the sights on it. Watched it. His breathing quaked. He let his finger from the side of the barrel and onto the trigger. He felt its cold iron taste the skin.

The sun began to flare up. A wind pushed over them. Some of the Guanaco became skittish and began to trot. The sentinel moved around towards where the men were prone, close enough that they began to worry it would give up their position. Newen hissed at the creature. Bernardo stole glances up from the scope of his rifle and saw the animal with its enormous black eyes staring. He looked back to the scope and saw the flash of beige. The Puma flung itself up as if on some great iron spring and onto the back of another one of the

Guanaco. It flipped around and kicked and the Puma fell and spun around and leapt again with its massive paws spreading across the shoulders of the beast that was some three times its size. The rest of the herd bolted across the steppe and towards the men. The sentinel turned and began to run towards the herd.

Shoot the sentinel, Newen ordered sharply.

Why?

It will bring the herd on us. Shoot it.

Bernardo eyed the scope and levelled it on the sentinel that had almost reached the herd some seventy metres away. He pulled the trigger. The animal stamped to the side and turned the herd to the east. He followed the sentinel and pushed the bolt to chamber another round and sighted the midriff. The Guanaco slowed. Bernardo held and let out a breath before firing again. The animal fell. The crack of the rifle sent the herd on a dozen metres before idling again.

Good kill, Newen said.

He moved the scope to where the Puma had been, and it was gone. There was a lone Guanaco heading across the steppe towards the herd. It was shaken but uninjured.

The Puma?

Gone, the old man said, rising. Let's skin this and take some for food.

Bernardo knelt in the grass while the old man went off. He turned his bag around and reached inside and took the box of bullets. He loaded the rifle with two more and then stared into the box. He counted only sixteen. He spent a while searching through his bag. Nothing. He must have miscounted. Sixteen bullets.

They spent most of the morning skinning and carving up the meat of the felled animal. They spoke only in small bursts. The old man showed him more effective ways to butcher a large animal and he was thankful for it. How much of this living he did not know surprised him. He wondered if this mission he had set for himself was doomed to fail for his own incompetence. One day with Newen and he had had sight of a Puma. Maybe it was the one he searched for, maybe not. But it was at least more than he had been able to find in weeks.

You just need to learn, Newen had said. It is not easy.

They caught up with the herd as the sun was highest. They sat out on the plain and ate raw Guanaco liver for lunch. Newen had foraged some wild plants to wrap the liver like parcels. Helps digestion, he said. They watched the herd in there graze. A new sentinel had been seamlessly appointed.

Do you have any ammunition, Bernardo said.

For that? Newen replied, looking down at the rifle.

He nodded. Felt a strange sense of shame for asking.

No. I don't use them.

What do you use?

I will show you the best way to trap if you like. It will be small prey though.

He nodded. Thank you.

Newen waved a hand. It is refreshing to me. Do you know many of my village are simply in the city now? They live like the white man. That is why I am no longer the Lonko. There is nobody to lead.

Bernardo was quiet for a while. They carried on eating. Watched the herd. Watched the wind flatten the grass in sheets. He pitied the old man. He saw a reflection of himself. What he might become. And just the thought made him uneasy.

Why did you go to England? Newen said. You could have gone to any place.

I wanted to forsake everything. This language we speak now. The people. I thought the farther the better. And my maternal ancestors were from England, you know.

They were?

He nodded. The Smiths, he said. I found out it was a common name. I always thought it was special because it was the name of my mother. Truth is, in those early years I regretted going there.

◆

The man at the dockyard reception office had accosted Bernardo from behind his desk. He had a massive black moustache and black eyes that held close together.

What's your business in England? Are you a Jew? How long do you plan on staying? Where are your documents?

To which Bernardo could say nothing, for he did not know the words. He simply shook his head.

Again the man asked him, louder this time. Bernardo shook his head once more. He pushed forward on the desk the papers he had stolen from one of the sailors aboard the *Bodegraven*.

The man inspected them. Where will you stay, he asked.

A thought came to the boy. He pointed to his own ears and shook his head. Another man came to him and pulled him aside and asked him more questions. He repeated the same method. Pointed to his ears and shook his head. I can't hear you, he had thought. If I can't hear you, you must help me.

Have you been examined by the doctor? On the ship?

Bernardo said nothing. The man sighed and folded the papers and handed them back to the boy and wrote down something in the ledger. Looked back up at him.

Twentyfour?

Bernardo nodded.

Go on then, the man said, shifting his head towards the exit.

And then he was outside again and the city of Liverpool awaited him. Almost instantly he felt a horrible sinking in his stomach. And a single question. What now?

He walked slum streets not far from the docks amongst buildings so tall and close together the sun would not reach him. He met others that lay in groups in full tattered and stinking suits as though they never knew when someone might want them for a job interview. In truth they were simply the only clothes they owned. They passed around brown bottles of dark liquid. Shared what they had with Bernardo and asked no questions. At night he sheltered in abandoned buildings of crumbling blue brick and balled his hands in his denim coat pockets and stood around street bonfires in old metal bins and pulled his collar up and hugged himself. He slept here there and wherever, with only drunkards and hungry rats for company.

They stayed with the Guanaco herd. You don't simply arrive and leave in the same day, Newen had said. You follow them. You are like their guardian in a way.

But it had been weeks and the Puma had not come. Bernardo had begun to doubt Newen. And the minute the doubt entered him like hot coffee on a cold morning it burned his throat and repulsed him. How could he not trust the man that had shown him a way of preserving his bullets? How to make more effective snares from willow wood? How to utilise them in the rivers and streams? How to better lay traps under the forest floor for rats and Culpeos?

When do you think another will come, he asked.

The old man furrowed his brow and shrugged. Who can say. This is a large herd. They are prime for hunting.

They reached the foothills of a mountain and the summer rains lashed down on them with whitehot anger. They set up their temporary camp half sheltered by a grove of twisting cypress trees. They dragged the tarpaulin across the width that separated two trees and tied it and from their bags pulled the blankets and laid them underneath. Then there they sat still beaten by windswept rain and watched the Guanaco stand as they always did.

That night they ate raw fish from the bone, for the wood around them proved too wet to start a fire. They spoke of the old days. Stories of Bernardo's paternal grandparents. Of the Mapuche and their plight. Of when he was a pup in the arms of his father.

I always knew you would grow up strong, Newen said. You had determination in your eyes.

I don't know about that.

Moving away to the other side of the world at fifteen? Fighting in the war? Returning with your boy and surviving as long as you have? Now you hold in you determination where others would give up. There is a possibility you may never find the Puma you seek.

I will never stop looking, Bernardo said.

See? Your father would be proud.

I want James to be proud. He was all I had to be proud of. I want him to have his justice.

You think your boy would want the Puma dead? You think he knows of revenge?

Bernardo did not answer.

Here, Newen said after a momentary silence, handing over a small cloth parcel. Bernardo took it.

What is it?

I made it for your little one. Before.

He unfolded the cloth to reveal a wooden figurine of a cat. Bernardo ran his fingertip down the front of it.

The following morning they stopped at the bank of a river. White water flurried around rocks. Newen knelt aside the river and considered the mud. Old Puma tracks, he said. Almost washed away.

Bernardo unhooked the rifle from his shoulder and held it at his waist. He looked around at the country. Early birds floated. The mountains dull and grey held commune over grey grassland. The rush of the river its only noise.

Newen followed the tracks down the river, bending down to frown and grunt.

What do you look for, Bernardo said.

Direction. Follow the tracks but imagine you are the animal. Where would you go next?

Over there, Bernardo said, pointing at the offchannel eddy that moved to the west.

The old man rose and nodded. Easier drinking over there for the beast.

Let's go.

The old man sniffed. No.

Bernardo turned to him, his rifle strap swinging in the motion. In this dawn half light he could scarce make out if the old man was smiling or frowning. Why, he asked.

This is where I leave you. I think this is something you must do for yourself. Don't you agree?

But the tracks?

They are old. Whichever Puma left them is long gone. Do what I told you.

Newen held out a hand and Bernardo took it and they shook. The old man's hands were cold and rough as steppe stones.

Good luck.

Thank you, Bernardo said.

No need to thank me yet. Bring me back a souvenir from the Puma.

He stayed by the river and watched the old man head off to return to his own life. To be fair, he had done enough. Still Bernardo felt a detachment. A reassurance Newen had given him. He stood watching the old man's figure shrink smaller as he walked away, and when he had lost sight of him through the western woods the sun had climbed from behind the mountains and turned the country green again.

THE cypress trees showed their first autumnal leaves. The grass was spent from relentless summer sun beatings over weeks past. Bernardo scoped the bluffs that forced themselves from the earth. He the proxy sentinel for this herd he had not left for more than a few days at a time throughout this new period of loneliness. He thought on what Newen had taught him. Stayed with the herd throughout the steppe and rose before the sun every day to catch a glimpse of something, anything, but came up short. The southern mountains watched from their icy peaks like emperors at a show and he felt himself thinning in both body and mind. Within him harboured doubt and hatred for himself and the Puma. Still he did not let the doubt overcome the hatred, and it was this hatred that pushed him farther into the wilderness every day, surviving on caught scraps of rats and fish not bigger than his smallest finger. He eyed the Guanacos with his stomach that turned over inside him, groaning. He made a ceremony of opening all the contents from his bag until he found at its bottom the box of bullets and counting them all and repeating to himself You need them for the Puma. You need them for the Puma.

After being in England for months he had become accustomed to living on little. He opted for movement. Place to place around the city he went with regularity, even if it was back to a place he had been only a few nights prior, it was new for that night, for he did not wish to seem part of a particular group. Mostly he went where the shelter and the food was and where the police were not.

There was the kitchen in the north of the city that served free soup to anyone: widows and street rats like him and everything in between. He waited in the line for over an hour. When he reached the counter he asked for bread and butter in his broken English. The server nodded and said, All get a barm love, don't fret.

She ladled white lumpy soup onto a shallow plate and poured water into a metal cup from one of the white jugs lined up behind the counter. She handed it over to him and smiled and he thanked her. She was pretty. An aquiline nose that poked out of her face.

Soft brown hair tied behind her white cap. Her skin unmarked and soft.

Next, she said.

When he turned to leave the counter he heard something he had hitherto not been witness to since stepping from the ship. A man came through from the back kitchen wearing a shirt and tie with a dirtied towel slung over his shoulder speaking Spanish to one of the servers. He stared at this man as other people pushed past him to get to the counter. Thick black hair and moustache. His olive skin made a presence of him amongst the pale white. He spoke to the servers with a coolness and they smiled and shied away from him. Bernardo could not quite hear what was being said as he ate away to the side of the building where men, women and children shared benches and small tables. After he finished eating he approached the side of the counter and shouted to the man in Spanish. The man turned and looked over the crowd until his eyes met Bernardo. Then he approached.

I need a job.

You are from Spain?

Bernardo shook his head. Chile.

Got papers?

I have sailing papers.

Good enough, the man said. His smile lifted his face. Come around the back, we will get you sorted.

You cannot speak Spanish to anyone back there. Okay? Only me.

Why?

They won't understand you.

He was put up in a boarding house with others from the kitchens. The first time he had had an English bed. He could finally see for himself a future in that country. Having so little for all that time started to seem worth it to him.

He rose in the middle of the night and found the air chillier with the changing of the leaves. A cold film stretched over his face like the most embryonic of ice sheets and he lifted his hands and rubbed it and held his nose. Well, now I'm up, he said, rising.

Stagnant air upon the land. The stream water was black, so black it reflected no celestial light. He found himself gazing above at skies grey with flat blanketed cloud as far as his gaze would reach. Bernardo turned back and saw the boy James. He was astride a rock by the stream. Looking down with his back to the man. His clothes hung in shreds like flesh from bone. Bernardo was bolted to the spot. The boy would not move either.

The wind made wrinkles of the stream and blew the boy's clothes away from him, revealing his body. It was as white as the moon.

James, the man said. Son…

He reached out but the boy did not turn around. He did not move at all. Only turned the wind like some lonely gravestone.

The following days the land was overcome by autumn, and wherever Bernardo went he took the boy with him. He felt the weight of the boy on his back. The chin on his shoulder. He felt cold breath wash his neck. He scoped the Guanaco and James asked him, Will you get it, Bernardo?

He caught a rock eel and roasted it on the open fire and James walked away from him and parted the grass like wind. He saw only the back of the boy. I am sorry, said the man.

A dawn like any other. The Guanaco herd had taken to resting not far from the man, as if they knew they were safer for his presence. Bernardo took a liking to them. He would watch them in their steady rising some hours before the sun would shine on the plateau. How they stretched their long necks. How they cut wet morning grass with their chisel teeth. How they shook their coats and made their strange laughing noises. They held close to each other. Something he admired about them. He saw in them something that had eroded from within him. Still he did not know if their togetherness would save them from a Puma. He had to remind himself what Newen had said. Eye the land around. If you were the predator, where would you come from?

He scoped the bracken of the steppe around the herd and saw nothing. Only darkness. Above: the skies plagued with cloud not even the brightest summer sun could penetrate. Suddenly from the herd a frenzy. The Guanacos' calm snuffed out in an instant. They ran across the plain to the west. Bernardo trained his sight on the herd and let the animals run through it. Nothing but heads bobbing and legs kicking up. He dragged his sight eastwards and saw a lone Guanaco with a monstrous Puma hanging from its neck. All four paws overwhelmed it and yanked it down into the brush. He aimed at them both, watching them wrestle for their lives. His heart leapt.

When he looked down the scope again the Guanaco was down and the Puma atop it with its massive paw across its prey's chest and mouth clamped around its neck. The Guanaco kicked out and calmed and kicked out again. He looked to the ears of the Puma. Is it you, he thought. Is it you? He could not see. Its head was rounded and its eyes were pulled open with wild desire, both ears pinned back. It looked to Bernardo the exact beast that had attacked them. That took James from him. James was next to him now. He whispered to the man, Will you get it? And the man said, Yes son, and he drove the bolt forward and aimed aside the clavicle and fired.

The crack of the rifle muffled the groans of the herd, splitting through the morning, and after it silence. The Puma had flipped off and away from the Guanaco. Bernardo could not see it.

He took only the rifle with him across the valley to where the ruin of the early morning was splayed across the grass. He shouldered it without aiming, but he was ready for the beast to jump from behind the mass of the Guanaco. With his knees bent he moved across the grass, almost in a glide. He reached the scene and felt the heat coming from the Guanaco. Its neck lolled over in the grass. Where there was but minutes ago movement and the jerk and twist of a mauling, a killing, now there was nothing. He peered over the top of the Guanaco in stages, with ease, with caution. Then he saw it. The Puma lying there with a torso of blanketed blood. It had been hit behind the shoulder and lay dead. Its muscles were relaxed. It looked like it was asleep save the tongue that fell from the side of its jaws. He squatted and lifted the head of the Puma. It was heavy and hot and had a stench not unlike freshwater fish. He inspected the ears. Both were unremarkable. He let the head fall into the grass again and looked around. The wind pushing against him. His eyes streaming.

He knelt aside the paralysed Guanaco. Its eyes wide and frightened. Its grunt like that of a birthing cow. Bernardo unsheathed his knife and drove it into the animal's heart. He got to work on skinning it and taking what meat he could carry. Of the Puma he did not know what to do, so he simply left it.

When the day was upon him and somewhere behind the blanketed cloud a sun was hidden he held staked Guanaco meat over the fire he had made for himself next to the carcasses. The herd had moved off long before. While cooking he looked across to the Puma time and time again. Half expected it to move.

You are not it, he said aloud.

He wished it was. Then all this would be over. But what would come after? He shook his head. A question that did not need an answer at that time. It was not the Puma he hunted, but he was glad for the killing of it. It was one less. It looked remarkably small next to the Guanaco. How this thing could be the cause of his pain he did not know. After he finished eating, he cut a tooth from the dead Puma and held it in his hand. He was glad it was his even though it was not the Puma he hunted. He would keep it as a motivator. May the next one be the one.

At a stream he squatted and refilled his canteen. From his pocket he took the Puma tooth and placed it in the clear shallow water and held his hand outstretched and let the water flow over it. The blood separated from it like red smoke from firewood. Against the tooth a wink. It glinted like a crystal. He looked up whereby the sun had begun to show through cloud.

He camped atop a rise in the land. The wind made a hard job of him setting up a fire, but in time he got one going and when he did he dropped the equivalent of a sapling on it. See the man: hillside with this bonfire like a beacon to the wilderness, a warning. I am here. I am come and I hunt the bones of those that wronged me. And he stared into this massive mound of flames a new person, all that had come before stripped away by what was. His eyes like globes red with desire. From behind the fire's dance formed the body of his boy. It snaked through the tongues of orange before lifting its head to view the man. A scornful face.

I am sorry, the man said. I failed you. It won't happen again.

A tree limb broke under the heat and crashed atop its own burnt bones and sent flurries of ember into the night. He watched them shoot up like tracer bullets. When he was alone in thought his current failure always found ways to remind him of those from his past. Guilt repeats itself.

He woke to sirens. He shot out of his bed and down the stairs of the bunkhouse he shared with eight other men. Outside, the docks of Liverpool were ablaze. He like others along the street was out and watching the smoke plume into the sky and soon the sky itself was red as hot iron and the blacked out buildings like stampings against it. Around the smoke the searchlights swerved. Around the lights tracer fire from antiaircraft weapons shot up in springs of white and yellow. A warden came walking past the narrow street shouting the people to their shelters.

His bunkmates, all men from the kitchens, came bursting out and down the street and made for the shelters. He frantically scanned the men that had moved out of the house.

Where is Robert?

He isn't here? one said, stopping. But almost as soon as he did a scream overhead and the earth began to shake. The man's eyes shot wide open like dishes of milk. An unforgettable look. He turned and ran away. Whistles blared. Wardens shouted, Be calm! More bombs fell. The smell of soot and smoke. The compressed air. Bernardo faced the door he had exited, and entered it again.

Up the stairs and across the far side of the room Robert lay unconscious. He turned the man over and set loose an almost empty glass bottle across the floor. Robert mumbled and waved his hand at Bernardo. He slapped the drunk and shouted Wake up. We are leaving.

Robert sprang from his bed like a rabbit released. He shot eyes around the place.

Where is everyone?

Gone. Now come on.

Is they at it with the bombs again, lad?

Bernardo had him by the shoulders and pushed him towards the stairs, but as they reached them the drunk shrugged him off and shouted My bottle.

Leave it, damn you.

Robert staggered across the room and bent to his bottle. Bernardo looked to the ceiling. A screaming shake. He shouted to Robert but it was no use. The roof of the building came down on them both.

Timber still alight woke him as it came down not six inches from his head. The red light of the sky showed where the roof of the bunkhouse used to be. Tracers flew like stars streaking across the night sky with delayed pops. In this moment he was sure he would die.

Bernardo rose in stages. Touched fingertips to his head and felt a warm ooze. Heat all about him. His ears rang. His mouth packed with dry white dust. He coughed it up and spat blood. The sirens still wailing. The bombers still screaming.

Robert, he called, stepping amongst the rubble. His voice sounded strange. He did not recognise it. The upper floor of the building was standing uneasy on its foundations. Up the walls curtains of fire were drawn and rising into the open air. A voice called from the rubble:

Bernie...

He moved aside some smouldering wood and coughed again. Robert, he shouted, but he could hardly see a thing. He knelt down and felt the floor shake. It seemed as though it could fall through at any moment. He heard the voice grow louder: Bernie... Bernie...

He grabbed bricks and threw them aside and with each brick the floor quaked. He jammed his hands into a gap between two beams and pulled. Above an approach from another bomber. Its wailing came for them like death itself across the crimson sky. Bernardo looked down and pulled the beams again.

Bernie, the drunk said. It was a lone red eye glinting in the firelight. A massive, startled eye. Help me, it said.

He looked up again and saw the aircraft. Felt its scream against the foundations of the house and in his own chest. Bernardo let go of the beams and ran down the stairs and out of the house.

It had been days without seeing the herd. A detachment inside him. He sat in the long grass as the wind blew away his tears. The man knew the herd was gone and there was no use carrying on after it. He did not know when exactly it had passed beyond his reach and felt more pain for the not knowing. Like the passing of the boy he could not stop or control it. He had to let it go. But this comparison of losses led him to where he last saw the Puma, where it had taken everything from him, and to work from there.

He travelled for days on end with the weight of the boy on his back. The wind pushed him back as if it was the earth willing him to not go back again to that place he had spent weeks returning to in spring. He knew it would probably yield no results but he went anyway, for he would have a keener eye for tracks and for movement. On the way the man tried to think of brighter times, when he and his boy had their bellies full of Huemul meat and chicken's eggs. But his mind made him relive the moment at the bluff.

When he arrived he studied the stone he had fallen upon. It was stretched out and deepset. He ran his hand over the flat of it. Cold and alone. He imagined it being in this place long before he or any other human had stood there. How small he was to the stone. How insignificant. He turned to where the Puma had attacked them. Eyed the land. The thick brush. The rises and dips. He attempted to manifest the beast. To will it to reappear ready to be slaughtered. He did this for hours, but the Puma did not come.

It was the distant flurry of brown that caught his eye. He shouldered the rifle for a better look. A Guanaco stepping with the alertness of a sentinel. And not far beyond it: the herd.

He slew a further five Pumas over the final weeks of autumn. They came in different guises and with different tactics to take the Guanaco, but his tactic remained the same. Silent and still as a stone. He took four with one bullet each but wasted a further three on the fifth beast. Seven shots in total since his resumed residency as Guanaco herdsman in the basin and beyond. He likened it to his very own arena.

James was next to him. Will you get it? he whispered to the man. And the man said Yes son and he drove the bolt forward and aimed aside the clavicle and fired.

Not one of them was the Puma he sought. Something he knew was more probable than not but still he felt his heart fall when each time discovering it true. With each one the boy James would run his small, almost translucent hand through the fur of the beast.

I know it is not the one, the man would say. I am sorry. But it is another one rid from this land.

He repurposed a length of tendon from the leg of the fifth Puma and tied each tooth together that he collected and made a bracelet of them. He scrubbed them in a stream and tried to wash the blood from his hands.

At twentytwo Bernardo had hauled one half of a stretcher across uneven French farmland turned over not by plough but by mortar shell. When someone went down, he and his fellow medic moved in. In this battle they did not have to wait long. They stumbled over at speed on the uneven ground. Around them tanks rolled, forcing bricks from houses and entire walls from barns and outbuildings. Bullets whipped through the air. The snap of the rifles was like a thousand hammers hitting brick all at once. They crashed down aside the fallen soldier. He was shot through the leg and blood pulsed from it and soaked his trousers and he held Bernardo and whimpered and shouted at him as if it was he who had put the bullet there and both the medics set about wrapping it and dragging him onto the stretcher. Immediately a call for help from across the field where it met the clusters of buildings. And another.

And this was how it was for him. He woke up and asked himself if he was the next to die. If that day was his day. In those early times of war he regretted joining in the first place. But he reminded himself. Remembered entering the office and telling them his want for revenge on the Germans on behalf of his mate Robert. The mate he had left as a desperate eye in that burning building.

You're lucky, he said to the lieutenant. This man far ahead of him in age and rank and here Bernardo cradled him as the other medic checked the shrapnel lodged in the man's back. And he knew the lieutenant was not lucky. After the man breathed his last they rolled him from the stretcher and went off again. They came to a group of three men. Always they had to make fast decisions. Leave the man with a bullet in the arm to attend to the one hugging his own guts. The screams stayed with him. The screams and the blood. They soaked his hands like paint. Not a speck of skin could be seen. After each skirmish he would wash them in buckets. But it proved hard to scrape from beneath his fingernails, so much so they began to stain pink.

Bernardo rose from the stream and headed back to camp. An early cold had set in. He shivered as he walked. When he arrived he went to work on sewing the Puma pelts together with a crude needle he had forged from rock. There he sat in the grass as those thousands of years before him might have. Living off what they could glean from it. For his supper he cut steaks from the Puma and grilled them over the fire and ate them steaming and juices fell from his chin and onto the pelts he blanketed over himself. The Puma had become his sole possession in this world and his sole purpose. It sustained him in body and mind. When he ate their meat he felt a small victory over them. A purpose fulfilled that fuelled him.

It was a biting cold morning when he rose as he always did before the moon was hidden and from the north came a black figure bobbing about the brush, a confident figure unconcerned with detection unlike any Puma he had hitherto seen and Bernardo knew, just knew what it was. Who it was. He knelt in the grass and studied it in his scope. It was far off, yet his trigger finger was already itching and his heart beating like that of a trapped rabbit. He followed it as it moved closer to the herd. He could see now in this dim light the thing was circling around its prey, and at that moment it slowed and lowered itself to barely the height of the grass. As it snaked around the ditches in the basin Bernardo moved closer. He too proning with the pelts held over him.

He came up about thirty metres from the beast. He trained the sights on it once more and focused on its head. It looked off to the side still. Bernardo could feel the breath of the boy like the wind.

Get it, the boy demanded.

I will.

He trained the reticle behind the clavicle. The Puma ceased its trail and rose on its legs and turned and looked directly at the man. From this distance it was an insignificant thing. No threat. Yet as his scope was met with the glare of the Puma, the Puma with a moon torn from its ear, the Puma that he had been hunting, Bernardo froze. The wind had ceased. The sound of the Guanaco, gone. The only noise was the crashing of his own heart. He fired the rifle.

The Puma was up in the air and off towards the edge of the basin. Bernardo fired again. Missed. He jumped up and set about running across the basin but halfway across turned back to collect his things. He knew he would not be returning. He was to abandon the Guanaco. He had no more use for them. He shoved everything into his bag and tied the tarpaulin in loose rags around it. Shouldered the bag. Loaded two more bullets into the rifle. Five now including the loaded ones. He left the carcasses behind for the condors.

He had tracked the Puma into the woods. He could smell it on the wind. Everything he had been waiting for was showing itself. His body shook. His teeth gritted and white foam spilled from the corners of his lips. He moved not on any form of fitness but on an instinctual desire for slaughter.

As he reached a brook that ran through the woods he stopped and eyed the tracks. They followed the water towards a rise in the land where a cluster of felled trees lay atop each other as if they were the piled dead from a battle ready for the grave. He followed the trail as the wind smothered him and he felt in his heart sorrow for what he was to do, not for the sake of the Puma but for the sake of himself. What would he do after killing the beast? What would he have? He set himself on his knee and shouldered the rifle but let its barrel rest in the leaves and watched the trees.

About the trees were black recesses like wooden caves. And from the central void showed the head of a Puma. It emerged like something new to this world but to Bernardo's eyes was at least a few years grown. Yet there it was with its two perfectly formed and unscarred ears. And from another void, another Puma. This one smaller.

Around the base of the trees stepped the beast he was hunting. It looked up at the trees and leapt on them to greet the others. They jumped at it and nuzzled it with their heads and pawed at it. They were but half the size of the adult Puma. Bernardo lifted the rifle to his shoulder and scoped it again. Scoped all three of them. He held the sights on the mother. He watched her as she descended from the trees and moved off southwards through the trees with the cubs in tow. Bernardo lowered his rifle. He felt the presence of the boy behind him. A soft breathing. When he turned to view it, there was nothing.

THE snow wrapped around the peaks like ponchos. Bernardo had fashioned himself one by cutting a hole in the sewn Puma pelts and he sat in that cold morning warming himself under it. His fire long out.

His gaze was taken from the mountains when the Puma moved in on a lone Guanaco. From his perch no more than a hundred metres away he watched them, knowing at any moment he could take a shot at the Puma. He did not. It was the cubs that stayed his hand. Yet every time he had the Puma in his sights, the boy James was prone alongside him, asking him that same question: Will you get it, Bernardo? To which he would reply: Not just now, son. For then and times such as those throughout the winter of 1955 the man followed and watched the Puma, and in his gaze saw the truth of it.

Then the Puma was atop its prey wrestling it to the earth and lay upon it, jaws clamped around its neck and eyes like great black moons. He saw its belly bulge with each laboured breath. This was but the second time he had seen the beast's success. He had taken some joy time after time he saw it fail to provide for its young. Not so easy in this place, is it? he thought. Is that why you resorted to trying to get me and my boy? Is that why? But now he only felt bitter. The Puma stayed on the neck of the Guanaco until the dawn had broken and Bernardo had started on what remained of his coffee.

The family of Pumas had previously stayed around the kill for a few days, making sure they stripped as much of the meat as they could. This time was different. They left it the same day with helpings of meat on it because another Puma came slinking across the steppe with a confidence as though the carcass was indebted to him. Bernardo knelt in the grass and eyed the beast. He chambered a round and thought about killing it. Then he lowered the rifle. If I had more rounds, you'd be a goner, he said aloud. He promised himself he would not waste them on prey other than his ultimate. Each time he watched the Puma stand over its kill as it fed its young he questioned when that day might be.

Bernardo was lucky. The Puma and its cubs were migrating south and did not waver much to any other direction. It seemed as if they were fleeing. This meant he could track them easily across the steppe. He held relief for the fact he had found them before they began this migration. They traversed lowlands and all their rises and dips and recesses. And they moved fast. Bernardo had no time to fish or trap or hunt anything. He stripped berries from trees and plucked late mushrooms from their bases. Over his shoulder the whisper of the wood. He gleaned what lay behind him. His wild eyes searching like lights.

When he came upon the mother Puma it had made another kill. A brown fox that had once been red. It was sat at the edge of a creek like it was drinking but it was dead and savaged. Its insides bored out and limbs stripped to the bone. The sinew stretched tight like a wire trap. He was in the lows of a tree, his riflescope downcreek. They did not wait around this kill either, and not long after the man found himself kneeling in the water breaking open the ribs and sucking the marrow from them. His hot breath plumed about the bones and disappeared into the late morning. He realised it was an old carcass and not one taken by the Puma. Riddled with maggots and stinking.

◆

But still the Puma went on across the steppe in search for sustenance and survival in the ever bitter days where the sun showed itself for what felt like a few short hours and then it was frostfilled wind and ash on the grass from the fires that needed to be built larger each day. And it was one of these days he viewed this family of Pumas lying reposed in the brush. The yellowed grass thin and swaying in the wind and the maroon bushes. The mother licked her cubs. They lay together even in times such as these and comforted one another and the man felt sorrow for the fact he had only himself to hold.

What even was there to hold? His arms were like twisted branches. His bones had begun to protrude from his shoulders. He moved his fingers between each rib and felt its rise and fall, a landscape all its own. He ran his hands down his leg. Pulled up his jeans and felt the icy wind move over the scars where the tibia had been pinned.

His second mission in France was one he wished he could forget. Operation Epsom, everyone was calling it. The men moved along the track that ran behind a hedgerow. It was a hot day and the sun seemed to linger for an age, rising in temperature with each moment and never holding still. They came to a clearing whereby they could see out through the hedges flat farmland until it rose at a line of trees. Instantly one of the men went down. Then a crack echoed across the field. The men spurted clear of the opening, rushing to flank the treeline. He and the other medic dragged the man that was hit to the side and knelt alongside him.

It will be all right, Bernardo said. But the man was already dead. Shot through the eye. The other eye was closed but the one that had been hit gaped open.

The shots whistled over the hedgerows. The men went down one after another. It was within the hour they were close to where the sniper fire had been coming from. They threw mortar shell and cover fire at the ridge before moving up. Bernardo stayed prone behind the lip of the hedgerow. John, the other medic, grabbed him by his jacket and screamed at him.

Come on.

Still he did not move. He saw a man that was not him rise from where he lay and run out onto the field with John and be shot through the chest. The air smoking from his back before going down and dying there in the mud in a country not his own.

Sod you, John said before rising alone with the stretcher half hauled underarm and half dragging across the floor.

Bernardo watched him run. He reached one wounded and started tending to him. Men ran past him either side to reach a hole in the land dug out by artillery, but as they reached it the ground shot up from beneath them. Flurries of soil skyward. A scatter of limbs. Bernardo looked back to John. He was face down in the grass. By then sniper fire had all but gone. Bernardo rose and ran across the field to John. Turned him over.

Oh God, the man said, looking up at Bernardo. He had been shot twice through the abdomen. Black blood washed out of his uniform. Bernardo pressed down on the wounds. Looked up. Landmines blew up out of the earth like geysers. He saw groups of men lying over one another. Men holding their broken legs.

Don't leave me, John said, grabbing Bernardo by the arms. Morphine. Morphine. Don't leave me. Tell my mother. Tell her…

John's head fell back into the earth. Bernardo dragged the stretcher up from the ground and went on towards the treeline. Men ran past him firing from their hips. Screaming. He moved towards a dip in the land where a cluster of men lay holding themselves. Before he could make it a thwack in his leg. Then he was on the ground. He crawled and in this crawl he thought he would be finished off. But he was not. He reached cover. Only then did he look down at his leg. Bent and broken. He reached for the morphine in his pack and bit the top off it and stuck it into his flesh below the knee. At the incline of the hole he rested his back. Looked around at the men. They were all dead.

He thought more than once of taking aim at the cubs. You took my young from me. I will take yours from you. Then he would see them play with one another again. He witnessed them grow stronger as well. Stalk one another with more ferocity. Their leap extending like a child's shift from walk to run. He even named them. Bob and Ben. Bob was the older more forceful sibling. He saw his own brother Jaime in Bob. Ben was closer with the mother. Always sleeping tucked under her chin or splayed across her back. Yet none of what he was weighing up was pertinent. He had watched the Puma fail again and again to make a kill. If she could not feed them they would die anyway. He made a pact with the Puma only he was privy to. If you do not eat, neither do I. Their fates henceforth bound. Moving in parallel like train tracks.

As his health declined so too did the weather. Snow fell with a fury across the steppe. One night, he dragged himself to a grove of malnourished trees in their twisting and set about making a camp. He took down limbs from the trees and made a small crude roof that he blanketed the tarpaulin over with great effort. His arms ached and his legs felt like they would give way at any moment. His body entire numbed by the cold and battered by snowflakes as large as stones. Don't weep by the mountain. Don't weep by the mountain. A sweep of silent wind sent the tarpaulin waving into the air. Bernardo the only thing holding it down with what remained of his strength. It blew and the flakes swirled and hit his face and he held his head down into the tree limbs and closed his eyes.

When the wind calmed he pulled the tarp back over the roof and tied it down at each corner. He packed thinner branches over the top of the tarp. He heard calls ride on the air. He put his bag inside the tent and walked to the edge of the grove and eyed the plain. The air swirled with quiet white. The sky like sheets. Breaking out from an eastern ridge was the Puma. It walked for a moment before stopping and calling out. The call that cut through the cold. He watched the figure of the Puma step with caution before stopping and sitting and then stepping again, her head dipping each time as if she was trying to remember something.

Too cold to make a fire. Too wet. He held himself in his furs under the tarp, wishing away the splitting hunger pains and listening to the snow collect on the outside. Muffled evermore with each passing hour. He shook and breathed hot air into his hands and rubbed his chest and pressed his fingers to his belly. In this state he thought he might not last until morning. Perhaps that would be better. What did he have if not the Puma's tooth? The one tooth he was yet to collect. He hated himself for waiting.

Outside the howling ceased and the night came but it was still bright as morning. He made a gap in the tarp and pushed his hand through. He grabbed a fistful of snow and pulled it inside and drank the snow down and gasped. Rubbed his chest with his free hand. When he reached out of the tent again he saw through the gap a pair of feet. A child's feet. He followed them up to the body of the boy, where he stood collecting the snow on his shoulders. Bernardo retracted his hand and pulled the tarp together and sat back and held himself again and rocked onto his side shivering.

When the snow had calmed the boy was no longer there. He lifted the tarp heavy with some four inches of snow and forced himself out. He straightened up and felt pain like claws raking over his skull. He felt his muscles wearing away. His body eating them in its desperate attempt to go on. He held out his hand and dipped forward, but a dread came over him and he worried if he sat he would not rise again.

The land was transformed. Buried. How fitting it would have been for him to be made a permanent frozen fixture of it. He would not have blamed it, this land. It was the god of his living now more than ever. Something he could not control or claim. But here he was, still a habitant.

The Puma was drinking from a river half frozen over with jagged sheets of ice like loose translucent mosaics. No cubs. Low winter sun tore over the mountains and scorched the snow. A sea of cold, bandaged desolation. Cut through it the slushed paw prints of the Puma. He followed them until he came upon a wide glacial lake surfaced by thin frozen films. He scoped the edge of the lake from east to west. Scoped it for a while and saw nothing. He picked up the tracks again and carried on, leaving behind two sets of prints in the snow, and if any witness were to come they might think he had walked with the Puma.

He scoped her moving across the plain. Another trailed not far behind. It was the larger cub, Bob. The long yellow grass pushed through the snow in sparse spikes. They walked through it flanked by the enormous granite mountains that burst from the earth. Bernardo lost the tracks. They disappeared down the land and amongst the snowbattered brush. He pressed on.

The foothills were surrounded by skeletonised trees black as though they had been burned, and sauntering around them was a flock of rheas. Birds, yet pulled to the floor for their size like Czech hedgehogs. The tracks of the Pumas moved off sharp to the east, where the land formed a hill and offered tree and bush cover. The slush webbed against the hills. The rheas tottered, some preening their wings, others pecking about the snowy ground. Their heads hidden and shown and hidden again. Their wings pulsing outwards intermittently. Bernardo watched them with fondness. A beautiful sight. The land was quiet save the sound of the snow coiling and melting where he stood.

Two Pumas burst from the snow and down the hillside towards the rheas. The mother ahead of the cub. Snow threw up like white smoke and fizzed in the air with their leap. Bernardo flinched as they went. He watched them extend their embossed leg muscles that ripped through their coats. The rheas screeched as they scrambled across the valley and shot over the edge of the hillside. They were chased out of Bernardo's sight by the Pumas and in their rush left behind only mist. He watched the land settle and quieten again before running down after them.

His form was awful. Each leg lifted up over the snow with great effort and then back down, toe first.

He felt his foot stick in something hidden under the coverage. His ankle rolled and he leant forward desperately and snatched his foot back out as he fell onto his side. A snapping like a twig underfoot. The soft doof of his landing. Then he was still. He gritted his teeth and sucked in the air. Do not scream, he whispered to himself through the pain. They will hear you. You will scare them off. He lay there in the snow and attempted to control his breathing for some time and aimed to do so until the pain subsided, but it did not. It only grew, and he moaned low and long like a birthing animal.

In that long ago when the world entire was at war he was laid out on a stretcher in the makeshift infirmary amongst screaming men refusing to die and quiet men resigned to it. He was neither. He was silent for his shame. He was seen to at the infirmary and told he had shrapnel in his leg and he asked them if he could return to the war and they said they did not know.

Days later he was visited by an officer and the officer held out his hand and Bernardo took it.

The officer produced a small box and opened it to show a medal hiding therein. The medal of something or other. Our medics are the best of us, the officer said. The truest heroes.

Bernardo turned over in his bed and retched. He wiped his mouth with the back of his arm and turned back to face the officer.

All right, chap? the officer said, covering the box again and setting it down at the foot of the bed.

I watched them die, Bernardo said.

You did your best for them. I know they were better off with you there to comfort them.

You don't understand.

Take the medal, son.

He lay in that bed for weeks and when he was recovered he was stamped unfit to return to the front. He was first contact for the returned wounded. He ended up serving in that same infirmary until the end of the war.

But not until the last day did he open the box with the medal inside. He took it out without even studying it and slipped it into the coat pocket of another doctor. It was not for the shame that he hated himself but for the fact he could not rejoin the effort and do better. Make amends.

He lay against the melting snow and felt a determination fill him. His breath steaming and his bones chattering. Shan't die here, he said aloud. His voice granitic. His ankle had already begun to turn black. He moved his fingertips along the swelling. He could not feel anything. For the cold or the injury he did not know. How desperate he had become. He felt ashamed. He pushed his bag back into the earth and lay down to rest his head on it. Above sheets of white. He felt his blood move.

He groaned as he sat up and turned and dragged the bag around his side and opened it. He took the machete and shuffled on his backside to the nearest tree and reached up to the base of a limb and began to hack at it. An insignificant slice. But one became two, and two four. And he went at the tree with what he could muster from his wasted arm until in between two strikes against the tree the hard compression of snow snapped. Bernardo turned to face it. The Puma cub. The smaller one, he assumed, but still from this close it surprised him with its size. He slowly took down his arm from the tree and held the machete outstretched. He said not a word. The Puma held its head low and faced him with one paw crunching in stages through the snow. Its pure white whiskers stuck out like needles. Its eyes like green fire. It was a beautiful thing. He had seen them close before, but only dead. Here he could see its ears twitching. Bernardo shouted at it. Vamos! Go! In his stupor he slashed the machete at the cub. It drew back its ears and hissed at the man. He waved his arms again and screamed at the thing as loud as his lungs would let him. It began to back away and he shuffled himself backwards and grabbed the rifle and brought it up and levelled it and fired. The white smoke of the gun waved into the air and dispersed with the exhale of the man. It revealed the Puma cub in the snow. A widening ring of red, silent as the land.

Bernardo was quiet for some time. He held the rifle pointed at the body even though his arms were shaking. The boy James was lying alongside it cold and bluelipped. Tears fell down the man's face. He let go of the rifle and held his own head. A gravelled moan that clawed at his throat like a bad cough. He shook his head each time he took a glance at the cub. He felt sick, but still he carried on through the force of his own body's want for survival, this body that became more numb with each passing moment in all that cold, this body that listened not to the torment of its mind or the aching of its spirit but to the needs of its blood and its skin and its stomach.

That night he gorged on Ben's liver. He tried to cook it over a fire it took him over an hour to build, but almost as soon as the scent of it sizzling in the pot reached his nose he took it out and held it steaming and bit into it. He took snarling bites and swallowed, barely chewing. He bent over and retched and sicked it up. How his body saw this food as something foreign after it had become so accustomed to eating itself. He went on with it slower this time, and in between heaving he swallowed and kept the liver down until it was consumed entirely.

Bernardo did not wait long before dragging himself to the carcass again and splitting its ribcage and taking Ben's heart. This time he diced and cooked it and could wait for it to brown before he devoured it. A warm salty taste he had not felt on his tongue in ages. He added more wood to the fire and reposed under the tarpaulin and hugged his full belly. Soon he was in his dreams.

And there was the Puma on the hill in a shining shroud like some angelic figure sent from above and he moved up the hill towards it with no clothes held around his bones. The man walked with the boy and Ben the Puma cub and all the other Pumas he had shot. Then he was aside the Puma in its shine and a queue formed and he watched them go to the Puma and enter its shroud and become absorbed by it and by the time the Puma had consumed all save the boy James it was a deep red like burst blood from a fresh kill and its eyes held black and stared at the man and past the man. On the hill was the man's father and the man's wife, Olive. She went on by both man and boy and he called out to her but no sound came for there was only wind and that wind carried over everything and soon Olive was consumed. Bernardo looked down to his side and the boy too was gone and he looked to the Puma massive and red and full of rage yet the man did not back away. Instead he followed those who had been consumed by it and went to the red Puma and wrestled it in his arms and fell down to the earth with it as it consumed him.

He woke in the night sweating. He pulled his hand from under the pelts he used for covers and moved his fingers about the palm. Warm sticky ooze. He sniffed it and turned his head away and held his hand to the fire. Sat up and wiped it away against the warm wet soil. He felt himself hard under the pelts and he was confused. Was it the sight of Olive in the dream, or something else? Inside himself a guilt and a sickness. Something that had not happened to him for months had happened in his dream of the red Puma.

Seeing Olive made him wish to see her in real life. The second time they had met she came to the foundry he had found work in. It was the autumn of 1948. At first he did not remember her face. She looked to him as many others did in this country, but as he considered her for a moment he noticed the cleft lip and the green eyes he had once seen reflected in morning sun.

She looked down in awkwardness. Don't you remember me?

What are you doing here?

She looked down at her own belly. He followed her gaze. There it was.

The light was failing when they went through the streets at a half walk. Bernardo could not bring himself to look down at it. That bulging belly that filled him only with fear. In fact, he spoke without looking at her at all.

What will you do?

What do you mean?

I mean will you keep it.

What choice do I have, it is mine.

There are places you can take it afterwards.

There was a silence for a while. The sound of their shoes upon the stone pavement. He still did not show even a glance at Olive. He realised she had tried to initiate a shared look more than once, but he was too frightened.

It is yours too, you know, Olive said.

Are you sure?

She stopped walking. He went on a few paces before realising and turning back to her. Then they shared a glance, short as it was, into one another's eyes and said nothing.

The third time they met was at Olive's house. One parent, three bedrooms and seven sisters. He sat through the lectures from the mother. The matriarch of the family. She spoke of timing and respect. Of duty and care. You are not ready. You barely know each other. You aren't married. You don't have a home together.

He looked around. Girls everywhere. Adult, teenage, toddler. The matriarch was enormous and imposing. All the while Olive sat quietly next to him. Their cool, naked arms touched.

What do you do?

Work in the foundry.

Your parents?

They aren't around.

Up north are they.

My mother died. My father is back home.

Sorry to hear that. Where is home?

In the Americas. I moved here when I was young.

Olive turned to him and frowned. You aren't English?

The grilling continued in such a way until Bernardo had proven some kind of worth to the matriarch by way of making some new life for himself in this country and serving it as a native would as well.

In the end the matriarch sat back and exhaled. She looked at Olive. Looked at him. Her eyebrows raised and the corners of her lips downturned and bottom lip poked out. She nodded.

They met by the Mersey. It was not even a week later and Olive looked so much bigger.

Grows fast, Bernardo said.

Too fast, Olive replied.

Did you think about it?

About what?

What I said. About him.

You don't know it's a him.

Does it make a difference?

Thank you for taking me out. I don't see the river often.

You don't?

She shook her head.

They went along the banks watching the water's flurried rippling. How even now in this weather that threatened to bring a storm it was still so much calmer than the days of the bombs.

Have you? Thought about it?

Olive spoke without looking at him. She kept her chin inwards. When I was little all me mates at school had dolls, little babies, you know? I never wanted them. I used to watch the teachers talking and wonder what it was they spoke about. What problems they had. Maybe somebody had died in the family, I don't know.

Why did you care about them?

Maybe their husbands had died. Or their grandfather, you know? And we're playing with dolls. Playing mum and dad. I couldn't stop thinking about how much they might be hurting at home. I didn't want to live in me own world. I had me sisters at home, who were babies too. They needed me.

What about your mother?

She couldn't handle them all, what with me father.

You were like a second parent to them.

Yes. Now I have to do it again.

You don't have to. There are places.

It's not right.

But you don't want it, I can see that. You shouldn't—

Olive lifted a hand to her face. Sniffed. Bernardo unfolded his arms and placed a hand on her shoulder. They stopped walking and stood there. The wind battered them, sending tears backwards upon her face to join her hair.

She makes me, Olive said.

Who makes you? Your mother?

Olive nodded. Hereby Bernardo saw her as she was, a frightened thing hardly a woman herself, with nobody but he to see it, someone she barely knew.

He rubbed her shoulder with his palm. It's all right, he said.

They found a table at a cafe and sat over a pot of black tea, its steam unfurling delicately in the cold air.

You are the oldest, Bernardo asked.

Olive nodded.

I am youngest in my family. We are different in this way. I always looked up to my siblings and one by one they left me. You haven't left yours. Your family sticks together. You should be proud of this.

But you want me to give away our baby.

I can see you don't want it, that is all.

Doesn't matter what I want. Never has. Stick together, me ma always says. Us girls stick together. I always have to be there for everyone.

She took not an eye from the tea. She looked lost in it. Consumed by it.

You won't leave us, will you? It's not proper if you leave.

He wanted to. But instead he took a sip from his mug and shook his head.

The next time they met they were wed. On the groom side: blokes from the foundry. On the bride: even more women. Cousins and aunties and friends. A simple ceremony. Reception in the pub they had met in. Cucumber sandwiches and cheese on sticks. A load of ale. Three fights. A slow dance. A kiss in the garden as if they were children and not just married. He had liked her face, her large eyes. But since spending time with her proper he grew to admire her. She did not want any of this and still she carried on. Did he truly fancy her? He thought so.

Do you like me? he said.

Her face was dark. Eyes reflecting red glow from the pub window. Was she smiling or holding back tears. She took his hand and led him back inside.

He recovered in the foothills. The snow his water source and Ben the cub his food. He carved up the carcass each morning. Tested his ankle on the short walks. Each step made him moan in pain but he dealt with it through sheer will to recover and find the Puma again. He yearned to see her and discover her fate. For all he knew she was dead of starvation already. Then I will find your bones and bury them, he said. Put an end to it.

It was nights of dreaming of the Puma in its redness and its merciless consumption of all he knew and days of reliving his time with Olive and coming to terms with how he found himself in this world.

This is Dr Bevan, he told her across the bedroom. The pair of them in the doorway. She was sat by the window.

You brought them here, she said, motionless in her nightclothes.

For your own good, Bernardo said.

Where is it. I want to see it.

James is downstairs.

Bring it to me.

Bernardo turned to the doctor and said, She's been like this for weeks.

I should have got rid of it when I had the chance.

What, Olive? Dr Bevan said, removing his hand from his pocket. What should you have got rid of?

The germ. Now it's out. And it's spoiling everything.

Why do you speak such nonsense, Bernardo shouted.

Don't you see it will take away everything? Everything we worked for. You and your fancies will ruin everything. Everything is ruined because of it and because of you.

Please, Mr Culpa. Let me alone with her for a few moments.

The look she gave him as the doctor approached. Ferocious black eyes glaring over shoulder. This once loving woman.

He stepped outside the room and shut the door behind him. There he stood like he was watching out for them, making sure nobody came. From inside the room he felt the deep murmurings of the doctor but nothing of Olive. He heard the whine of the baby and headed off down the stairs and as he did he heard Olive laugh. Not a crazed sort. It was a sound he had not heard since before she had the boy and he felt sad for the hearing of it and yet in turn a deeper sorrow for feeling that way about hearing her kind laugh in the first place. As he took the boy up in his arms and rocked him, the doctor came down the stairs.

Well, Bernardo said.

She needs plenty of rest. It takes a toll on the body is all.

He stepped closer to the doctor holding the baby against his chest. He almost whispered the words. You can see her, doctor. Hear the way she speaks. It is not normal.

She is tired and stressed. If it gets worse, come to the practice again. The doctor lifted his sleeve to view his watch. I best be off anyway. Take care.

The inlaws would visit. The mother, the sisters. In these days Olive would descend the stairs in stages, holding onto the banister with both hands. The inlaws would take turns holding the baby and smiling at it and dipping their heads while saying Hello, Hello. Aren't you a sight. Yes you are. Yes you are. But Olive would not dare look at it. And the man would watch her with a fist in his throat. Simmering like water in the pan.

She'll take to him soon. I couldn't stay awake for any longer than an hour for days after me first.

It's been months, Bernardo said.

She'll take to him, won't you Olive?

Who? Olive said.

◆

The sun rose early one morning on the hills and the fire was out thanks to the soft dripping from the tarpaulin where the snow had begun to thaw. He pushed back the pelt covers. On hands and knees he shuffled to the edge of the tarpaulin and held out his tongue and felt its cold drip. When he emerged from his shelter he propped himself up on the stick crutch and stretched out his back. Birdsong filled his ears. He leant on the crutch and lifted his bruised ankle and made circles with his foot while sucking air through his teeth. Still had some time to go, Bernardo thought. Stewed long enough here though, he said aloud. And he had. In this place he had thought of the past and dreamt of what afeared him for too long. He had to find the Puma.

Everything was packed. He stared at the body of Ben the cub. Carved and used. Something like a fallen tree riddled with sickness and ready to rot. He stood looking at it for some time. The cubs were the reason he held admiration for the Puma, the main reason for its survival and in turn its purpose for living. And he had taken one. Maybe that equalled them.

He thanked the cub for saving him and turned off around the hill. But the man did not get far before going back. He found himself there again looking upon the body of the cub. It would not do being out here like something unwanted and forgotten. He unhooked his bag and fell to his knees moaning in pain and fetched the machete from his bag and drove it into the hard earth. Hacked at the ground and dragged it towards himself and drove it down again. Gradually the soil began to loosen.

When he had a grave a few feet deep he grabbed the cub by what was left of its limbs and pulled it into the hole. It was stiff and cold. The smell awful. Flies about his face in their fury had had their turn. Now it was for the worms. He raked the soil over the cub until it was covered. Then onto that he lay broken tree limbs and any stones he could find. Cold and quiet the land took in the cub. Then it was done and he sat back and sighed.

Bernardo followed remnant tracks until he came to a forest wide as the plain it stood in. The tracks led inside before becoming sparser. As he followed what he thought had been left behind by two Pumas he doubted himself. Perhaps they were not left by anything other than the wind. Or some other Pumas. And if they did belong to those he hunted he knew not the age of the tracks.

He came to the carcass of a rhea. It was fragmented and riddled with parasites. It had been picked apart by animals other than those he followed. Above the canopy the high sun burst through thin streaks of cloud. A sun he had not been sure he would see but now when he felt its rays kiss his forehead he was thankful to be alive. He went on, the crutch helping him over stones and the machete cutting away at any brush that might have stopped him.

Some creature was hunched over amidst the trees with the head of some animal through his legs and he worked on it with a hacksaw. The scraping of the blade stole around the woods. Bernardo stopped and shouldered the machete and steadied himself on the crutch. It was a man. He wondered what to say. Whether to say anything at all. Just walk away. Go on. Nobody need know of your presence. Then the man working on the animal lifted his head. He wore a red cap and had even redder cheeks. His eyes from this distance were like little black beads. Bernardo stood holding onto the crutch.

Hello, the man said.

Bernardo eyed him without speaking. He eyed the animal. Some antlered beast. The hacksaw embedded in its skull.

What are you doing out here? the man with the hacksaw continued.

Is that a Huemul?

Yes. Why are—

Why are you going at its antlers like that?

The best part.

You can't eat them.

Of course. They buy them.

Who does?

People. I don't know.

Bernardo approached the man. He realised the man was only young. A boy even. Then he looked off down the woods behind the boy, where he could see figures walking to and fro between the trunks. The hollers. The hacking and chopping.

How many are there of you?

Are you all right, sir? Are you hurt?

What are you doing here?

We're working.

Working.

The boy nodded and then dropped the head of the Huemul. It made a tinny sound, almost echoed, as though it had been hollowed out.

Ramon can help you.

This is a Huemul. They're rare.

We have killed many of them. Wait here. I will get Ramon.

He grabbed at the string that held the machete around his shoulder and flung it about before the boy. Levelled it at him and whispered No. The boy stopped

and held out his hands as if in prayer. Perhaps he was.
Don't get anyone, Bernardo said.

All right. Be easy, sir.

How many are there of you?

A dozen. But there's more twenty miles down. And then there's a camp.

And you all kill the Huemul.

We have to make a living, sir.

Bernardo turned and spat into the earth and looked back at the boy. Do you all kill Pumas, he said.

If we get the chance. Of course we do.

Seen any recently?

Ramon did.

Who is Ramon?

My boss, the boy snapped, as if Bernardo should have already known it. He began to back away. Turn his head. There's no need for this, sir. We can get you help.

Wait. Do not get them. I am talking to you. Where was the Puma?

Ramon said he saw it.

Where did he see it?

You can ask him.

I am asking you. Where did it go?

West, I think. Let me go and ask him. Don't worry, sir.

As soon as the boy turned away to his mates, Bernardo had dropped the crutch and started off westwards hacking away any brush that stopped him. He went with a hurried limp like some frightened dog. The wild land unbroken and uneven. He fell down and struggled to rise again, groping at tree trunks and the brush that surrounded their stumps. Shouts came not long after. Long calls of words he could not make out. He could not tell whether they were after him. He did not look back to discover it. He went on.

Bernardo staggered through tracks the Puma had walked some hours prior. The wind forced him back and more than once he tripped, but it was a necessary diversion away from the hunters. Those cruel bastards. They do not kill the Huemul to survive, they are only money to them. He regretted fleeing from them, if only to grab them by the shoulders and say What in God's name are you doing? What is this? That animal he bet his and James's life on. That he managed to take only one the entire time of their being there. And how it still pained him he wasted most of it to the rot. He saw now why they were so much scarcer than when he had been a boy, and perhaps why the Puma was struggling also. He had to find her again and feared she might be already dead or dying. If they had spotted her as they did him, she could well be injured. He told himself he was alive, so she had to be.

He rested his ankle every now and then, and with each rest he pulled up his trouser leg and observed it. It had worsened with the walking. Wide black bruising around a swell of fluid buildup, soft to the touch. He pinched it and winced and his head fell back and in silence he cursed the land. He spent the night under the cover of thin platelike stones that overlapped one another to form a small ridge in the steppe. He managed to light a fire amongst the damp bracken. He stared at the fire for hours and wished for some guide or provenance as to where he would find himself in the dawn. He found nothing in the flames, for they were just that, flames.

In his search he found signs of the Puma but no sightings. He did what he could on one good foot and the broken one deteriorating day after day. And with it his health. He ate bits of carrion and sucked river snails from their shells. He had loaded another bullet into the rifle, leaving him but one spare. Perhaps one clean kill on a Guanaco and he could set up for some days, at risk of losing the Puma for good. He tried not to think such things, but maybe he already had lost the Puma.

His ankle had become so swollen it had doubled in size. He decided to set himself against a stone and take a blade to the swelling. Thick outpour of blood and pus. He let out a low groan and white spit burst from gritted teeth.

He limped through woods until he found some canelo leaves. He chewed them in his mouth and made a paste. Their peppery hot and sweet flavour reminded him of his childhood, of home. He thumbed the chewed paste along the incision before wrapping his ankle in a strip of cotton taken from his own shirt. The pain was still there. A thump not unlike a heartbeat, but followed by a seething scrape like a thousand nettles tasting his skin.

By night the approaching cries of foxes reminded him of home. How similar they were to those that he had heard ringing out over the streets of Liverpool. He sat awake one night listening to them and remembering that time. It was the night James had turned one.

He pulled the thin curtain away from the window. There it was. The reason James was crying the house down sat under the lamplight reaching its jaws into the air and rhythmically screaming. Short measured pops like polite gunfire. He held the baby to the window and pointed to the fox and said Look, it's just a fox, it's calling its friends. But the baby did not stop whimpering and crying and gasping for breath. He bounced the boy on his hip and said It's all right, it's all right. And the boy would not stop. And Olive was in the room and she was holding her hands to her ears and whining and speaking so fast the man could not understand her. He simply turned his back and opened the curtain once more. Look, he said, it's just a fox.

It was with the first germs of spring that he saw her again. She appeared from nowhere, as though she had always been there within reach of his scope. His mouth held open slightly. He attempted to swallow in a dry throat. His finger curled. His mind flooded with doubt. He only had three rounds, could he be sure this was the one? And where was the cub?

He rose and shouldered the rifle and headed towards the Puma. His ankle had hardly improved. It still bled and he felt it pulsing with pain in every waking moment, so much so his teeth had begun to wear away with the grinding. Out here he found no solace for these pains. It is life's way of telling us we're alive, his father always said. Spoken as if it was a good thing, this pain. Bernardo never agreed. It was seeing the Puma that filled him with an energy and made him feel alive again.

The Puma was travelling at some speed. She was not running nor did she seem like she was fleeing, but with each leap onto a stone or rise in the land and the subsequent drop back down she gained distance from the man. He followed as best he could, as fast as his ankle would let him. He could not lose her again. Twice he stopped and levelled the rifle and thought about firing, yet stayed his hand. Where was she going? She looked measured and determined. And well fed. Was she looking for the cub he had already buried? Did she seek her own revenge on the man himself, unknowing of his trail? But she moves south, he said aloud. His voice almost shocked him, for he had not heard it in days. He sounded different, old.

The Puma moved up a hill peppered with massive bulbs of bushes showing their first buds of green. There she stood inclined like some statue fronting an English manor. Bernardo had to gain on her. He pushed himself, past the pain and through the thoughts of any of this being worthwhile. He knew it was she for the way she moved, her slenderness, her beauty of coat that shimmered under any light. Still, he took no chances of mistaking her for another. He moved in closer as she prowled upon the precipice of the hill. He had to take the shot. To take it for his boy and be rid of it all for good. Then the Puma descended her pedestal and was lost from his sight. Bernardo stood motionless for a moment. He held in him unending frustration yet also felt some strange relief. A surge of wind rolled down the hill and pushed him back. It was the land telling him to flee, he thought. Be gone and end this another way. Let it go. Instead he dropped his head to the wind and braced himself against it, picked up and went on as fast as he could, scrambling over uneven brush and bramble. The hill against him, the wind against him, but stopping was not an option. He did not know the outcome of all this, save that quitting was not one of them.

Atop the hill he hunched over holding his knees, panting like a dog. His foot an agonising weight. A thought entered his mind that he would be better off without it, lighter at least. He lifted his head and caught sight of the Puma moving off towards the mountains. The massive stretch of metamorphic rock, old and scarred and capped a thin white like flashes of bone amongst skin. And above them loomed enormous clouds that looked closer to the consequences of artillery than natural formations.

The Puma went off towards the peaks that dwarfed her. He lifted the scope once more and saw it. Ahead of his Puma was another. He could not tell whether it was the cub or not. Bernardo poised for a moment.

Watching. Moving the scope from Puma to Puma. Make your decision. Make it now.

He trained his sights on the rear Puma. The one he knew to be her simply by the way she walked. He fired. The shot lifted rock dust from the mountainside. The crack of the rifle moved through his body, shook his bones. The grass below moved with the wind. The bullet missed not even by a small margin. The pair of Pumas propelled themselves about thirty feet across the mountainside in a jump and scramble. He ejected the empty shell from the chamber. He knew now he had to be fast.

Bernardo went on in that hobble that had become his walk, grinding his teeth, making crow's feet of his eyes. His movement more desperate now. He struggled in his attempt to move with all that he had brought upon himself. He must carry it as he carried the loss of his boy and his family.

It was not the other cub. It walked with an authority that could only mean it was a dominant adult male. The female Puma followed it throughout the rest of that day along a river, white with its rush. He scoped them sauntering about the foothills. They met one another yet still stood a few feet apart. The male approached without looking at the female and the female opened her jaws and showed fangs. He backed away and circled and tried again. They sniffed, watched, considered one another. Then the female lowered her head and nuzzled the male. Then they circled and embraced one another. Tails up. Each of them showing their fangs and hiding them and showing them again. The female lifted her paw to the sky for a moment. The male loomed over her as she fell to the earth under the mountain and looked up. Then she let her paw fall and sat there looking off towards the setting sun. The male positioned himself behind her. He moved slow and deliberate. As he lowered she rose and walked a few feet from him and stood. His back arched and head down with ears back. He lifted a great paw to her back and pushed her down. She lowered and they repeated this dance until darkness came. Bernardo knew he had too few opportunities and so he waited for the perfect moment, a time when he could be sure his failing body would make the shot. He set himself a fire and slept.

Olive held the boy James over a plinth of burning wood. She held her hands to her ears and screamed without sound. The boy atop the Puma, his arm a white pendulum lolling at the beast's side. He tried to reach out but his body was moving farther and farther away. And the Puma cub Ben was warm again and atop the man licking gently at his ankle. Cut it out, Olive whispered to him. It should have never been there. Cut it out. And he tried to yell to her but his voice was blocked, the screams hitting nothing and muffling and falling back on themselves and inside him. This yet another night he woke breathless and weeping. He did not know whether killing the Puma would rest and soothe his mind, but he had come to terms with the fact that he had to find out.

He tracked them to the edge of a mountain lake where the land reached up like some enormous rock wave in constant threat of falling upon them all. He imagined it crumbling down. How their ruin would be hidden for aeons and nary a traveller would know it. He looked away off to the eastern side. The rock was sparse of any vegetation so he spotted them right away, even in the copper dawn they moved in. It was the male following the female this time. And each time the female rested he would lower himself upon her, only for her to rise again.

And they went on for hours, at all stages of the sunrise. They stole along the foot of the mountain, past turquoise pools, under rock overhangs, these two Bernardo could not take his eyes from for the feeling of missing some minute detail of their courtship, a flicking ear, a tentative sniff of the air, a rising shoulder blade, a flash of yellowed fang or the flicking of a tail.

His ankle was seeping a solution of blood and pus. Time to time he stopped and pinched around the fracture and felt the pain slipping away into numbness and he thought about stopping for his dizziness, whether from lack of food or for the infection he did not know, but he would scope the Pumas in their locomotion and become infatuated again. Constantly he was in this strange state where the Puma both angered and enticed him. As Olive had before the end. Someone he would watch with fondness of memory but pain of present nature. Yet here it was the opposite. He watched them with interest as one might watch the waves on a beach or the leaves on a tree or shadows dying in sunset, and held in him the pain of the past. What this beast had done to him, had taken from him. Yet still that pain and fury at this animal was but a veneer to what he knew to be his true sickness.

The Pumas stopped halfway up an offshoot of rock peppered by freshly sprung brush and bramble. Their golden coats like barley amongst the greens. They had become closer than before and the female did not shy away. It seemed to him, placing his sights upon them both from the mountainside, that she had finally given in and accepted the advances of the male. He was only partly right.

The male moved in on its prize, but whether for the sharpness of his great clawed paws upon her back, or the aggressiveness of his thrust, the female whirled where she lay and opened her great jaws wider than the man had seen before, and lashed out at the male. Bernardo shuffled closer along the rock, not taking an eye from them. Blows were exchanged. The female flipped over and landed again on her back as those evil paws of the male lashed across her face. A mass of red. The dust rising. These blows so onesided Bernardo assumed it an assertion of pride now, and once that was established again the male would be off. But he did not leave. He continued his assault. He imagined the pain of each wound searing across skin. In this moment he saw the life of the Puma he had been hunting for all this time in the hands of this male, and so he did not scrutinise his actions but hastily aimed upon the male's midriff and shot him.

By the time he arrived at his kill, she was gone. He looked down at the site. Grey rock painted deep red, almost black. The shallow pools and splashes covered in thin films of dust that had settled and dulled their sheen. The male Puma lay dead with its tongue dropped out of the side of its splayed jaws, the fur around them matted with dried blood and upwards to its eyes flecks of red like some crude warpaint.

Bernardo held out the rifle and turned over the head of the beast with the barrel. Its eyes like wells without water. He could not remember killing a Puma of this size before. Still his satisfaction came in not the killing of this Puma but the saving of the other. The image of the Puma lying under a barrage of blows held in his mind. A helpless mother with no way of salvation in this wild other than he. Only then did it occur to him to discharge the empty cartridge from the rifle, leaving just one left.

He made camp of the kill site and dropped a diced steak of his kill into the small skillet. The calls of the foxes rode on night winds that traversed the mountain. He saw the moon's pale white disc upon the lagoon to the east. From the site it was but a small ring around the moon so perfectly centred it resembled an eye. He nursed his ankle with hot water. He poured it on warm but felt nothing so simmered it steaming and tried again. A sensation like fresh blood flushing down the skin.

Bernardo picked at the diced meat but could not eat it. He was soon hunched over vomiting into the dust. Then before long his entire body was on fire, and so he rid himself of his furs and slipped off his jeans. How easy they came down now without even needing to be undone. Then he was naked about the fire like some sweating hairless ape.

Throughout the night he repeated this undressing and dressing. Tossing about the dust and rock freezing and overheating all at once. He drank small amounts of water between naps but never fully slept, for the shaking of his bones would not allow him. This and the apparitions upon the mountainside. They came as shadows before forming in their full flesh and blood and coloured by daylight amongst the surroundings of indigo night. One the boy, a sight he was accustomed to seeing, but here the boy was older than he had ever been in life. His arms and legs extended and gaunt and pale. Yet his face was still his own. Ungrown and innocent. He stood without word, as if waiting for someone. Bernardo watched from his stupor, his head pressed against the earth with eyes pushing up and straining and his head streaming and his jaw shaking. There came Olive and she was half defaced by darkness and her body almost twisted and she held a hand to her ear. Bernie, she said, holding the ear. Bernie, why? Her words lost to the whistle and spit of the fire and these facades lost to darkness. And he stood there again in that tiny bedroom of their tiny home in the north end of Liverpool and he lifted the boy and held the boy's head to his chest and there Olive was screaming and he checked the boy over and said where does it hurt and the boy said nothing and he pulled the boy into his chest again and shouted back at her but he was drowned out by her raving, this speech of a mad person he was frightened of, truly as frightened as he had ever been and she held the hammer at her side and came towards him and he took off down the stairs and dropped the boy onto the settee before turning to her as she came halfway down the stairs already lunging at him, a picture of madness, reaching for the hammer with his left hand and striking with the right and she was against the stairs holding her ear and he held the hammer and she was bleeding from the ear saying the same thing over and over, Why, Bernie, why? but he did not stand there for long, he was with his boy James, who was only ever seen as his, who was the only thing he could do right by, who was seen as nothing less than a parasite by his mother, who was already swelling and bruising about the head from where the hammer had laid into him, who was lifted up again by his father and taken outside, the outside held by dusk light and the comings and goings of commuters and other children, this outside punctuated by shouts of mothers and the sounds of car horns and engines and the clop of horse hooves, here the man Bernardo who holding his boy to his chest looked for some aid but instead found stares and in this noise he did not hear the window unhook and swing open, and in this dusk light he did not see her as anything but a black shape drop onto the pavement no more than five feet from them both and lay there unmoving and twisted, the flash of white bone from the neck and the crowd of passersby growing and shouting almost instantly, but he, Bernardo, just stood with the boy James pulled into his chest.

He woke in the chill of the mountain with a grey ash pile where his fire had once been. A steel dawn unbesotted by the spring glow you might expect upon the steppe. His entire body wet and freezing. He reached for the furs and pulled them over him. He was in immense pain. Across the ash pile sat his father. He smiled at Bernardo. Here you are, he said.

Father.

Hello, son.

I think I am dying.

You will only die if you wish to.

I feel I must.

What for? Your grief?

Bernardo attempted to swallow in a dry throat. Shook his head. Grief, he said, is a feeling for someone else. But I don't care what the dead feel, how they felt while they were dying. I only care how it makes me feel. I feel sad because of grief. I feel sick because of it. I punish myself and I cannot see those I have lost. I am all that remains and I am all that matters. Why am I the only thing I think about? My pain. All while I am still living. It is they that died, they that should have my heart, but it is not. It is only myself I live with, not grief.

When you are gone, you are rid of everything. I do believe that.

But I did not kill the Puma.

Across the pile of ash the old man was smiling.

What? Bernardo said.

So you chased the Puma to make yourself feel better. Did it? You will kill the Puma to make yourself feel better. Will it?

I don't know.

Did killing the others?

No sound save the morning wind that shifted the ash and dust about them and Bernardo's breathing like that of a soil sifter.

The Puma is the Puma and the mountain is the mountain. This world knows nothing of your family, your life. Just as you know nothing of it. Killing it will not change that. Set yourself free of this sickness and come to me. I always wanted you with me, that's all.

Bernardo lay back on the cold earth and watched thin shreds of cloud waste away overhead. He felt his heart beating slow and heavy, his breath shortening. He reached for the rifle. Lifted his head and turned. His father was gone. He pulled the rifle to his chest and closed his eyes. Found the trigger.

♦

It was a calm day on the sea when they arrived at Valparaíso. The land showed itself for the first time since his boyhood. A flood of fear and excitement swelled in Bernardo, but he could not show it. He had to protect James. He had to show him there was promise and wonder to this new life. He looked upon these shores not as he did the British shores, as a foreigner, but looked upon them with familiarity and wonder, like seeing an old friend again, even though he had been but a child when he last spirited them. Now he returned and with him another bit of him and a whole load of reckonings and reunions to be done. What would they say to him? Whether they would forgive him or not was not a concern. It was only in his mind to see them and say something like It's been a while. Here, look what I have become. But to them he would not be a failure, he would not be fleeing. He would have the boy and he would have proof of a proud life abroad, earned for himself, built from the pits of homelessness and war and work. Bernardo watched these approaching lands with great optimism. There came the rush of nerves and excitement once more. His body became lighter. Everything, a sight, a smell, a noise to his ears, heightened. A euphoria that burst from his bones. He was returning home. He had told the boy it would be great, and he believed it. Seeing the land, his people. Showing his father what he had done for himself. Showing James a new world.

Look, so wide! James said.

Bernardo pointed out to the land and said, That is only what your eyes can see, the land goes for thousands of miles that way and that way.

James turned to him, their eyes level for the height he held the boy at, his eyes shining the colour of the sea. It's home time, he said.

That's right, son.

Home, he thought. Wasn't Liverpool home? Doesn't James know it to be too? Bernardo wondered if the boy could know the man's worry at starting again, at meeting his own father once more, of fleeing and returning all at once. Still, seeing the boy's excitement and hearing his simple words filled him with joy. This trait of the boy's was something the man always held in high regard. Even at such a young age, he always knew what to say to cure his father's worries. This was something Bernardo did not know he himself or anyone else around him possessed.

He refused to sorrow the boy for what had come before. He knew he must be the father he himself had for but a short amount of time before that old man had been changed and lost. The death of his own mother had caused that change, so he promised himself he would not do the same to James. He knew he must be even more grand, even more kind, even more inspiring for the boy now. Something that when he gazed upon the approaching land of his childhood he felt confident in his ability to provide. He would show his father what a good father does after all the structures of family come down and fail you. Are you looking forward to seeing Grandpa?

Yes, James said.

He wondered if the boy even knew what he was saying. He would not blame him if he could not comprehend. All Bernardo had known was big family and big country, all James knew was small and smaller.

They rode the bus from Valparaíso to Aisén. The boy sat windowside watching the rocky mountains go by.

Do you like this place? Bernardo said.

I like it.

Look up there, can you see the condors? Aren't they fine?

They are little planes, Father.

They look small in the sky, but they're larger than you.

Larger?

They're this big. Bernardo made a gap in between his hands the size of a condor.

They will eat me!

Don't be silly, they won't eat you.
You will stop them.
I won't let anything hurt you.

The coldness of the iron around his finger made the shaking worse. He opened his eyes again, removed his hand from the rifle and lifted it to his mouth and blew, but his breath did not help warm the fingers for it was cold, as was his blood. He ran his hand back down the bones of his torso, his muscles like dead tree limbs against the foothills, the ribs sticking from his skin like stones from riverbeds. As his hand met the trigger guard he slotted his finger inside. Now he needed only to push, push once and forget, and as he fetched the strength to do it, he felt the wind move odd upon him. A smell of soaking fish came with it. He turned his head in haggard stages. The bramble scratched about ten metres from him. There sat the Puma. Her head red with blood from the fight. She looked upon the slain male and the almost dead man. Her gaze moved from the two. She sat facing the mountain. That barleycoloured coat, that fiercely scarred head. The ear half taken. She was there for him. A tooth hung low from her jaw, and after watching her struggled movement he saw she was gravely injured. Almost the entirety of her lower jaw hung loose and bobbed about like a fishing float. He unearthed his body that was already half consumed by this ancient rock and turned onto his front. The remains of his muscles tightened, his mouth dry as clay, his hands shaking, the rifle shaking. He lifted it with great pain and anger, aimed it at the Puma, and fired.

Hours passed. The sun hid behind pale cloud. He had been dragging himself inches at a time along the mountain with the last of what he had in him, closer and closer to the Puma, who lay on her front, paws stretched out as if she was asleep, but her eyes held open and her heart had stopped beating. And when he reached the head of the Puma he stopped. He turned half on his side, writhing in pain, until his eye met her eye. There, bathed by midday light, in the eye of the Puma he saw a true reflection of himself.

In the dawn there is a gaucho at the edge of the lagoon. He dismounts the horse and washes himself and waters the horse before mounting the horse again. He moves on and with him his herd that he and his dogs are ushering through the mountains. He holds on his personage all the land they move upon, and below that land the bones of all that came before and claimed ownership at one time or another now belong to him also. He yells to the dogs and shouts them on and they whirl around the flock, snapping at them and pushing them on.

Across the edge of a small bluff an odd shape pulls his gaze and he rides the horse up and over the sparse mountain path until he comes to the remains of a Puma, all but bones stripped by this land and all that dwell in it. And aside the Puma a collection of furs tied together.

From them a recess in the earth like something dragged across it. The gaucho kicks his horse on and follows the trail of separated brush and dust until he comes to an overgrown thicket bursting from the rock, and amongst it the lonely bones not of another Puma, but a man. It too ravaged by all that walk this land. The gaucho dismounts and squats aside the bones. Considers them. The clothes but weatherworn torn rags spread around the earth like manmade bramble. Around the base of the skull some strange protrusions. The gaucho reaches for them and lifts up a small link fabric chain with yellow Puma fangs attached to it.

Not far from the bones lies a rifle that looks more like a large stick. The gaucho rises and steps around the bones and retrieves it. A bolt action. He struggles with the mechanism but grits his teeth and sets the stock against the earth and pulls down on the bolt until it ejects one round onto the ground. He fetches it up and hums, considering it before dropping it into his pocket and remounting. He lifts the hat from his head and holds it to his chest for a moment before replacing it and kicking the horse on once more. He moves off down the foothills alongside the dogs and through the valley, pushing on his herd, before breaking through the western mountainside and leaving all else behind.

ACKNOWLEDGEMENTS

The author wishes to thank Jordan Mulligan, Jack Ramm, Sarah Terry and all at Swift Press for their hard work in helping to realise this novel.

He also wishes to thank Paris, Kim, Patrick, Michael, Stephen, Jo, Emma, Joan and the Sinclairs for their continuing support.

Lastly, endearing thanks goes to the natives of Patagonia and their organisations such as Fundación Patagonia Natural for preserving the habitat of the creatures contained therein.